# Penelope Fitzgerald

was one of the most elegant and distinctive voices in British fiction. She was the author of nine novels, three of which – *The Bookshop*, *The Beginning of Spring* and *The Gate of Angels* – were shortlisted for the Booker Prize. And she won the prize in 1979 for *Offshore*. Her most recent novel, *The Blue Flower*, was the most admired novel of 1995, chosen no fewer than nineteen times in the press as the 'Book of the Year'. It won America's National Book Critics' Circle Award, and this helped introduce her to a wider international readership.

A superb biographer and critic, Penelope Fitzgerald was also the author of lives of the artist Edward Burne-Jones (her first book), the poet Charlotte Mew and *The Knox Brothers* – a study of her remarkable father Edmund Knox, editor of *Punch*, and his equally remarkable brothers.

Penelope Fitzgerald did not embark on her literary career until the age of sixty. After graduating from Somerville College, Oxford, she worked at the BBC during the war, edited a literary journal, ran a bookshop and taught at various schools, including a theatrical school; her early novels drew upon many of these experiences.

She died in April 2000, at the age of eighty-three.

From the reviews of *The Beginning of Spring*:

'The story spans a few weeks, yet it evokes a whole life. An astonishing amount of research has been effortlessly incorporated. Moscow is seen and smelt. In splendid vignettes, Penelope Fitzgerald conveys the complexity of its denizens, their strangeness and charm, in elegantly simple, flawless prose. She conveys too the inconsequences of life and all that is curious and fascinating in human relationships. She is wonderfully witty – it is impossible not to laugh out loud. This is a marvellous, intelligent and beautifully crafted book.'

Monique Charlesworth, *Daily Telegraph*

'*The Beginning of Spring* is a charming, unexpected and deceptively simple novel. The surface of the book is so pleasing that the careless reader could glide over it happily without troubling to listen to its undercurrents. At a time when so many novels promise so much more than they deliver, it is agreeable to come on one that does the opposite. The picture of Moscow is completely realised. Reading the book offers the same pleasure as turning over an album of old photographs ... There is a gentleness and good humour to the life she portrays which are rare qualities in contemporary fiction.'

Alan Massie, *Scotsman*

'Reading Penelope Fitzgerald's remarkable new novel is like finding the roaring torrent of a great literature distilled into a clear, elegant glass. I have never seen more brilliantly evoked a Russianness which Russians themselves cannot describe because they take it utterly for granted. She has written a fitting fable for the age of perestroika.'

Virginia Llewelyn Smith, *Harpers & Queen*

'This, her latest work, has something of the grandeur of Balzac, and a similar overview of life as a human comedy with little logical plot development and fewer rational explanations . . . One cannot deny Fitzgerald's ability to engage and hold the reader's attention. I found it impossible to skim or skip for fear of missing a subtle piece of gossip . . . Compulsive.'

David Self, *Literary Review*

'She can sum up people in a single sentence that begs as many questions as it answers, but which is worth pages and pages of analysis.'

Victoria Glendinning, *Observer*

'With interest in Russia now so fashionable, a delicate, intelligent and readable piece of fiction like this cannot fail to please. It would only be a pity if popularity diverted attention from the high quality of Penelope Fitzgerald's writing, which must make *The Beginning of Spring* one of the outstanding novels of the year.'

Lesley Chamberlain, *Times Literary Supplement*

'Penelope Fitzgerald's skill lies in conjuring up worlds so intensely imagined that they seem like a dream, yet so real that you feel you were there, at their busy throbbing centre, only yesterday . . . No one is better at drawing with a few slight strokes characters who are more genuine for being unpredictable and who need time to work their surprises on us.'

Jackie Wullschlager, *Financial Times*

'This quiet but fascinating novel, one of the best I've read this year, is written with a pellucid style and a superb eye for detail, right down to the "Dundeekeks" which are to be found in a Moscow tea house. This is a novel I shall re-read with pleasure.'

Ian Rankin, Scotland on Sunday

'Her characters' dialogue is full of non sequiturs and off-the-point elaborations about love and religion, just like real human communication. In her books whole communities come to life, their ambitions and regrets all carefully noted by a wise and all-seeing Recording Angel.'

Sunday Times

'How is it done? How could she know so much about the minutiae of dascha housekeeping or the rituals of hand-printing craft, or the habits of Moscow nightwatchmen, or the nature of the entertainment at the Merchants' Club? . . . The plot may be inexplicit, but it is told with a virtuoso storyteller's technique, is illuminated by classic moments of comedy and keeps one (as the old blurb-writers used to say) guessing from the first page to the very last line.'

Jan Morris, Independent

'The Beginning of Spring can be adjudged a complete success. Fitzgerald's style is cut carefully to the size of her thought so that one has a constant sensation of a real intelligence never having a quarrel with itself in what it creates. In short, she persuades us, for the length of this quite exquisite text, to accept the world on her own terms, which are individual and intense, never mere echoes of someone else's sensibility . . . I reckon a fair number of readers will see no need to withhold their tears.'

Robert Nye, Guardian

'It requires considerable courage for an English writer to enter Russian territory made so familiar by the great writers of that land. It requires equal skill to pull off so bold an act, and Penelope Fitzgerald is triumphant on both scores. In *The Beginning of Spring* she has succeeded in writing a novel which does not feel as if it is written by a mere visitor to Russia, but is actually of Russia. Such authenticity may be the mark of the true novelist, but it is remarkable all the same when it works so flawlessly. This extraordinary book is Mrs Fitzgerald's best to date . . . No wonder, with this rare, riveting and highly mysterious novel, Penelope Fitzgerald is on the Booker shortlist yet again.'

Angela Huth, *Sunday Telegraph*

'*The Beginning of Spring* is a surprise, and something of a tour de force. The great messy city, muddling towards its destiny, is conjured up in vivid and astonishing detail: the narrow back streets with their seedy basement workshops; the crowded markets and railway stations; the exuberantly noisy club where the merchants drink tea and vodka; the vast dark river choked with broken ice and rubbish.'

Margaret Walters, *London Review of Books*

'Scrupulously well written, subtle in its effects, and feels completely authentic. *The Beginning of Spring* opens out into something more than you might expect.'

Hermione Lee, *Observer*

Also by Penelope Fitzgerald

EDWARD BURNE-JONES
THE KNOX BROTHERS
THE GOLDEN CHILD
THE BOOKSHOP
OFFSHORE
HUMAN VOICES
AT FREDDIE'S
CHARLOTTE MEW AND HER FRIENDS
INNOCENCE
THE GATE OF ANGELS
THE BLUE FLOWER
THE MEANS OF ESCAPE

# *The Beginning of Spring*

## PENELOPE FITZGERALD

Flamingo
*An Imprint of HarperCollinsPublishers*

Flamingo
An Imprint of HarperCollins*Publishers*
77−85 Fulham Palace Road,
Hammersmith, London W6 8JB

Flamingo is a registered trade mark of
HarperCollins*Publishers* Limited

www.**fire**and**water**.com

Published by Flamingo 2003

16

First published in Great Britain by Collins 1988
Previously published in paperback by Flamingo 1989 and 1996

Copyright © Penelope Fitzgerald 1988

This novel is entirely a work of fiction. The names,
characters and incidents portrayed in it are the work
of the author's imagination. Any resemblance to
actual persons, living or dead, events or localities,
is entirely coincidental.

ISBN 0 00 654370 7

Set in Postscript Monotype Spectrum by
Rowland Phototypesetting Ltd, Bury St Edmunds, Suffolk

Printed and bound in Great Britain by
Clays Ltd, St Ives plc

# The Beginning of Spring

# 1

In 1913 the journey from Moscow to Charing Cross, changing at Warsaw, cost fourteen pounds, six shillings and threepence and took two and a half days. In the March of 1913 Frank Reid's wife Nellie started out on this journey from 22 Lipka Street in the Khamovniki district, taking the three children with her — that is Dolly, Ben and Annushka. Annushka (or Annie) was two and three-quarters and likely to be an even greater nuisance than the others. However Dunyasha, the nurse who looked after the children at 22 Lipka Street, did not go with them.

Dunyasha must have been in the know, but Frank Reid was not. The first he heard about it, when he came back from the Press to his house, was from a letter. This letter, he was told by the servant Toma, had been brought by a messenger.

'Where is he now?' asked Frank, taking the letter in his hand. It was in Nellie's writing.

'He's gone about his business. He belongs to the Guild of Messengers, he's not allowed to take a rest anywhere.'

Frank walked straight through to the back right hand quarter of the house and into the kitchen, where he found the messenger with his red cap on the table in front of him, drinking tea with the cook and her assistant.

'Where did you get this letter?'

'I was called to this house,' said the messenger, getting to his feet, 'and given the letter.'

'Who gave it to you?'

'Your wife, Elena Karlovna Reid.'

'This is my house and I live here. Why did she need a messenger?'

The shoe-cleaning boy, known as the Little Cossack, the washerwoman, who was on her regular weekly call, the maid, and Toma had, by now, all come into the kitchen. 'He was told to deliver it to your office,' Toma said, 'but you have come home earlier than usual and anticipated him.' Frank had been born and brought up in Moscow, and though he was quiet by nature and undemonstrative, he knew that there were times when his life had to be acted out, as though on a stage. He sat down by the window, although at four o'clock it was already dark, and opened the letter in front of them all. In all his married life he couldn't remember having had more than two or three letters from Nellie. It hadn't been necessary – they were hardly ever apart, and in any case she talked a good deal. Not so much recently, perhaps.

2

He read as slowly as he could, but there were a few lines only, to tell him that she was off. Coming back to Moscow was not mentioned, and he concluded that she hadn't wanted to tell him what was really wrong, particularly as she had written at the bottom of the page that she wasn't saying this in any way bitterly, and she wanted him to take it in the same spirit. There was also something about keeping well.

They all stood watching him in silence. Not wishing to disappoint them, Frank folded up the page carefully and put it back in the envelope. He looked out into the shadowy courtyard, where the winter's stack of firewood was down by now, to its last quarter. The neighbours' oil lamps shone out here and there beyond the back fence. By arrangement with the Moscow Electrical company, Frank had installed his own twenty-five watt lighting.

'Elena Karlovna has gone away,' he said, 'and she has taken the three children with her, how long for I don't know. She hasn't told me when she will come back.'

The women began to cry. They must have helped Nellie to pack, and been the recipients of the winter clothes which wouldn't go into the trunks, but these were real tears, true grief.

The messenger was still standing with his red cap in his hand. 'Have you been paid?' Frank asked him. The man said he had not. The guild were paid on a fixed scale, from twenty to forty kopeks, but the question was whether he had earned anything at all. The yardman now came into the kitchen, bringing with him a gust of oil and sawdust and the unmistakable smell of cold. Everything had to be explained to him all over again, although it must have been his business earlier on to help with Nellie's luggage.

'Bring some tea to the living room,' said Frank. He gave the messenger thirty kopeks. 'I'll have dinner at six, as usual.' The thought that the children weren't there, that Dolly and Ben would not return from school and that there was no Annushka in the house, suffocated him. This morning he had had three children, now he had none. How much he would miss Nellie, and how much he did miss her, he couldn't tell at the moment. He put that aside, to judge the effect later. They had been considering a visit to England, and with that in mind Frank had cleared the family's external passports with the local police station and the central police department. Possibly when Nellie signed her passport it had put ideas in her head. But when had Nellie ever allowed ideas to be put into her head?

Reids, when Frank's father had set up the firm in Moscow in the 1870s, had imported and assembled printing machinery. As a sideline he had acquired a smallish printing business. That business was pretty well all Frank had left. You couldn't do anything with the assembly plant now, the German and direct import competition was too strong. But Reid's Press did well enough and he had a reasonably satisfactory sort of man to do the management accounting. Perhaps, though, 'reasonable' wasn't, in connection with Selwyn, quite the right word. He had no wife and appeared to have no grievances, was a follower of Tolstoy, still more so since Tolstoy died, and he wrote poetry in Russian. Frank expected Russian poetry to be about birch trees and snow, and in fact in the last verses Selwyn had read to him birch trees and snow were both mentioned pretty frequently.

Frank went now to the telephone, wound the handle twice and asked for the Reid's Press number, repeating it several times. Meanwhile Toma appeared with a samovar, the small one, presumably suitable for the master of the house now that he was left on his own. It was just coming to the boil and gave out a faint chatter of expectation.

'What are we to do with the children's rooms, sir?' Toma asked in a low tone.

'Shut the doors of their rooms and keep them as they are. Where's Dunyasha?'

Frank knew she must be about the house somewhere but was lying low, like a partridge in a furrow, to avoid blame.

'Dunyasha wants to speak to you. Now that the children are gone, what is to be her employment?'

'Tell her to set her mind at rest.' Frank felt he sounded like a capricious owner of serfs. Surely he'd never given them much reason to worry about their jobs?

The call came through, and Selwyn's light-toned, musing voice answered in Russian: 'I hear you.'

'Look, I didn't mean to interrupt you this afternoon, but something's happened which I didn't quite expect.'

'You don't sound altogether yourself, Frank. Tell me, which has come to you, joy or sorrow?'

'I should call it a bit of a shock. Sorrow, if it's got to be one of them.'

Toma came out into the hall for a moment, saying something about changes to be made, and then retired to the kitchen. Frank went on: 'Selwyn, it's about Nellie. She's gone back to England, I suppose, and taken the children with her.'

'All three?'

'Yes.'

'But mayn't it be she wants to see . . .' Selwyn hesitated, as though it was hard for him to find words for ordinary human relationships, '. . . might one not want to see one's mother?'

'She didn't say so much as a word. In any case her mother died before I met her.'

'Her father?'

'She's only got her brother left. He lives where he's always lived, in Norbury.'

'In Norbury, Frank and an orphan!'

'Well, I'm an orphan, for that matter, and so are you.'

'Ah, but I'm fifty-two.'

Selwyn had a reserve of good sense, which appeared when he was at work, and unexpectedly at other times when it might almost have been despaired of. He said, 'I shan't take much longer. I'm checking the wage-bill against what the pay clerks are actually handing out. You said you wanted that done more often.'

'I do want it done more often.'

'When we've finished, why don't you dine with me, Frank? I don't like to think of you sitting and staring, it may be, at an empty chair. At my place, and very simply, not in the heartless surroundings of a restaurant.'

'Thank you, but I won't do that. I'll be in tomorrow, though, at the usual time, about eight.'

He put the mouthpiece back on its solid brass hook and began to patrol the house, silent except for the distant rising and falling of voices from the kitchen which, in spite of what sounded like a burst of sobs, had the familiar sound of a successful party. Ramshackle, by Frank's standards, and roomy, the house consisted of a stone storey and on top of that a wooden one. The vast stove, glazed with white tiles from the Presnya, kept the whole ground floor warm. Outside, towards the bend in the Moscow river, a curious streak of bright lemon-yellow ran across the slate-coloured sky.

Someone was at the front door, and Toma brought in Selwyn Crane. Although Frank saw him almost every day at the Press, he often forgot, until he saw him in a different setting, how unusual, for an English business man, he looked. He was tall and thin – so, for that matter, was Frank, but Selwyn, ascetic, kindly smiling, earnestly questing, not quite sane-looking, seemed to have let himself waste away, from other-worldliness, almost to transparency. With a kind of black frock-coat he wore a pair of English tweed trousers, made up by a Moscow tailor who had cut them rather too short, and a high-necked Russian peasant's blouse, a tribute to the memory of Lev Nikolaevich Tolstoy. In the warm room, with no ladies present, he threw off the frock-coat and let the coarse material of the blouse sink down in folds around his lean ribs.

'My dear fellow, here I am. After such news, I couldn't leave you by yourself.'

'That's what I would have preferred, though,' said Frank. 'You won't mind if I speak out. I'd rather have been by myself.'

'I came on the twenty-four tram,' said Selwyn. 'I was fortunate enough to catch one almost at once. Rest assured that I shan't stay long. I was at my desk when a thought came to me which I knew immediately might be of comfort. I got up immediately and went out to the tram stop. The telephone, Frank, isn't the right way to convey such things.'

Frank, sitting opposite, put his head in his hands. He felt he could bear anything rather than determined unselfishness. Selwyn, however, seemed to be encouraged.

'That's the attitude of a penitent, Frank. No need for that. We are all of us sinners. The thought that came to me didn't concern guilt, but loss, supposing we think of loss as a form of poverty. Now poverty, or what the world calls poverty, isn't a matter for regret, but for rejoicing.'

'No, Selwyn, it's not,' said Frank.

'Lev Nikolaevich tried to give away all his possessions.'

'That was to make the peasants richer, not to make himself poorer.' Tolstoy's Moscow estate was only a mile or so away from Lipka Street. In his will it had been bequeathed to the peasants, who, ever since, had been cutting down the trees to make ready money. They worked even at night, felling the trees by the light of paraffin flares.

Selwyn leant forward, his large hazel eyes intensely focused, alight with tender curiosity and goodwill.

'Frank, when summer comes, let us go on the tramp together. I know you well, but in the clear air, in the plains and forests, I should surely come to know you better. You have courage, Frank, but I think you have no imagination.'

'Selwyn, I don't want my soul read this evening. To be honest, I don't feel up to it.'

In the hall Toma appeared again to help Selwyn into his sleeveless overcoat of rank sheepskin. Frank repeated that he'd be at the Press at his usual time. As soon as the outer door was shut Toma began to lament that Selwyn Osipych hadn't taken any tea, or even a glass of seltzer water.

'He only called in for a moment.'

'He's a good man, sir, always on his way from one place to another, searching out want and despair.'

'Well he didn't find either of them here,' said Frank.

'Perhaps he brought you some news, sir, of your wife.'

'He might have done if he worked at the railway station, but he doesn't. She took the Berlin train and that's all there is to it.'

'God is not without mercy,' said Toma vaguely.

'Toma, when you first came here three years ago, the year Annushka was born, you told me you were an unbeliever.'

Toma's face relaxed into the creases of leathery good-will which were a preparation for hours of aimless discussion.

'Not an unbeliever, sir, a free-thinker. Perhaps you've never thought about the difference. As a free-thinker I can believe what I like, when I like. I can commit you, in your sad situation, to the protection of God this evening, even though tomorrow morning I shan't believe he exists. As an unbeliever I should be obliged not to believe, and that's an unwarrantable restriction on my thoughts.'

Presently it was discovered that Selwyn's brief case, really a music case, crammed with papers, and stiffened by the rain of many seasons at many tram-stops, had been left behind on the bench below the coat rack, where the felt boots stood in rows. This had happened a number of times before, and the familiarity of it was a kind of consolation.

'I'll take it in with me tomorrow morning,' said Frank. 'Don't let me forget.'

# 2

Up till a few years ago the first sound in the morning in Moscow had been the cows coming out of the side-streets, where they were kept in stalls and backyards, and making their own way among the horse-trams to their meeting-point at the edge of the Khamovniki, where they were taken by the municipal cowman to their pasture, or, in winter, through the darkness, to the suburban stores of hay. Since the tram-lines were electrified, the cows had disappeared. The trams themselves, from five o'clock in the morning onwards, were the first sound, except for the church bells. In February, both were inaudible behind the inner and outer windows, tightly sealed since last October, rendering the house warm and deaf.

Frank got up ready to do what he might have done the evening before, but still hoped wouldn't be necessary, to send off telegrams. Then, at some point, he had better go to the English chaplaincy, where he could see Cecil Graham, the chaplain, and count on his saying, out of embarrassment, very little. But it would also mean an explanation to Mrs Graham, who in fact, did both the seeing and the saying. Perhaps he might wait a day or so before going to the chaplaincy.

At a quarter to seven the telephone rang, jangling the two copper bells fixed above a small writing desk. It was the stationmaster from the Alexandervokzal. Frank knew him pretty well.

'Frank Albertovich, there has been an error. You must come to collect at once, or send a responsible and reliable person.'

'Collect what?'

The stationmaster explained that the three children were deposited at his station, having come back from Mozhaisk, where they had joined the midnight train from Berlin.

'They have a clothes-basket with them.'

'But are they alone?'

'Yes, they're alone. My wife, however, is looking after them in the refreshment room.'

Frank had his coat on already. He walked some way down Lipka Street to find a sledge with a driver who was starting work, and not returning from the night's work drunk, half-drunk, stale drunk, or *podvipevchye* – with just a dear little touch of drunkenness. He also wanted a patient-looking horse. On the corner he stopped a driver with a small piece of resigned, mottled face showing in the lamplight above his turned-up collar.

'The Alexander station.'

'The Brest station,' said the driver, who evidently refused to give up the old name. On the whole, this was reassuring.

'When we're there, you'll have to wait, but I'm not sure for how long.'

'Will there be luggage?'

'Three children and a clothes-basket. I don't know how much more.'

The horse moved gently through the snow and grit up the Novinskaya and then turned without any guidance down the Presnya. It was accustomed to this route because the hill was steep and so a higher fare could be charged both down and up, but it was not the quickest way to the station.

'Turn round, brother,' said Frank, 'go the other way.'

The driver showed no surprise, but made the turn in the middle of the street, scraping the frozen snow into grey ridges. The horse, disconcerted, braced itself, crossing its legs and moving with the awkwardness of a creature disturbed in its habits. Its guts rumbled and it coughed repeatedly, sounding not like a horse, but a piece of faulty machinery. As they settled into a trot down the Tverskaya, Frank asked the driver whether he had any children himself. His wife and family, the driver said, weren't with him, but had been left behind in Rovyk, his village, while he did the earning. Yes, but how many children? Two, but that they had both died in Rovyk when the cholera came. His wife hadn't had the money, or the wits, to buy a certificate to say that they'd died of something else, so they'd had to be buried in the pest cemetery, and no one knew where that was. At this point he laughed inappropriately.

'Why don't you send for your wife to keep you company?'

The driver replied that women were only company for each other. They were created for each other, and talked to each other all day. At night they were too tired to be of any use.

'But we weren't meant to live alone,' said Frank.

'Life makes its own corrections.'

They would have to pull up at the back of the station, in the goods yards. The driver wasn't one of the smart ones, he hadn't a permission to wait at the entrance.

'I'll be back soon,' Frank said, giving him his tea money. The words meant nothing except general encouragement, and were taken in that spirit. Snow was lightly falling. The driver began to drag a large square of green oilcloth over the horse, whose head drooped towards the ground, dozing, dreaming, of summer.

The yard was served from the Okruzhnaya Railway which made a circle round the entire city, shuttling the freight from one depot to another. The sleigh had arrived at the same time as a load of small metal holy crosses from one of the factories on the east side. Two men were painstakingly checking off the woven straw boxes of a hundred and a thousand.

Frank walked past the coal tips and the lock-up depositories through the cavernous back entrance of the station. Inside the domes of glass a gray light filtered from a great height. Not many people here, and some of them quite clearly the lost souls who haunt stations and hospitals in the hope of acquiring some purpose of their own in the presence of so much urgent business, other people's partings, reunions, sickness and death. A few of them were sitting in the corners of the station restaurant watching, without curiosity or resentment, those who could afford to order something at the gleaming rail or the buffet.

The stationmaster was not there. 'The *nachalnik* is in his office. This is the refreshment room,' said the barman. 'Quite so,' said Frank 'but didn't his wife come in here earlier, with three children?' — 'His wife is never here, this is not her place, she is at his house.' The waitress, tall and strong, elbowed him aside as she lifted the flap of the bar and came out. 'Three little English, a girl with brown hair and blue eyes, a boy with brown hair and blue eyes, a little girl who was asleep, her eyes were shut.' — 'Did they have a clothes-basket?' 'Yes, when the little one sat down she put her feet on it, her legs were still too short to reach the ground?'

'Where are the children now?'

'They were taken away.'

The waitress folded her arms across her bosom and seemed to be challenging Frank, or accusing him. Her accent was Georgian, and it was folly, he knew, to think of Georgia as a land of roses and sunshine only. But Georgians pride themselves on their rapid changes of mood. Frank said, 'In any case, you are not to be held responsible. In no sense was it part of your work to keep a check on everyone in the refreshment room.' Immediately she yielded, becoming anxious to please.

'They're not your children, I can tell that. You wouldn't let them arrive like this in the city without anyone to take charge of them.' Frank asked where the stationmaster lived. His house was in the Presnya, between the cemetery and the Vlasov tile works.

He recrossed the swept and wheel-crushed snow of the coal yards. The horse was standing, entirely motionless, in the white distance, the driver was coming out of the urinal. He agreed to wait while Frank walked the short distance to the Presnya.

Along a side-road patched with clinker, carriage springs, scrap iron punchings and strips of yellow glazed tin which once advertised Botkin's Tea and Jeyes' Fluid, wooden houses stood at intervals. They were raised by two wooden steps above the ground and Frank saw that the entrance, as in the villages, would be at the back. At No. 15, to which he'd been directed, the back door, in fact, was not locked. He shut it behind him, and was faced with two doors.

'Who is at home?' he called out.

The right-hand door opened and his daughter Dolly appeared. 'You should have come earlier,' she said. 'Really, we have no business to be here.'

Inside, the table, covered with oilcloth, had been shoved into the right hand corner so that no-one could sit with their back to the ikons and their glimmering lamps. Annushka was asleep on the clothes-basket, Ben was at the table looking at a newspaper, the *Gazeta-Kopeika*, which dealt entirely with rapes and murders. He looked up, however, and said, 'When you're on a main line, the distance between posts is a twentieth of a verst, so if the train does that in two seconds you're going at ninety versts an hour.'

'What happened?' Frank asked. 'Who's looking after you? Did you get lost on the way?'

A dark woman in an overall came in, not the stationmaster's wife, if indeed there was such a person, but, as she explained, a kitchen-mother, called in to help as required.

'She only gets eighty kopeks a day,' said Dolly. 'It's not much for all this responsibility.' She put her arm round the woman's waist and said in caressing Russian, 'You don't earn enough, do you, little mother?'

'I'll settle up with everybody,' said Frank 'and then

straight home to Lipka Street. We shall have to wake up Annie, I'm afraid.'

The children's outdoor clothes were airing above the stove, along with the stationmaster's second uniform, and a heap of railway blankets. Hauling down the birchwood clothes frame was like a manoeuvre under sail. Annushka woke up while she was being crammed into her fur jacket, and asked whether she was still in Moscow. 'Yes, yes,' said Frank.

'Then I want to go to Muirka's.'

Muir and Merrilees was the department store, where Annushka scarcely ever went without being given some little extra by the astute floor manager.

'Not now,' said Dolly.

'If it hadn't been for Annushka,' said Ben, 'I think Mother might have taken us on with her. I can't be sure, but I think she might.'

The whole house began to shake, not gradually, but all at once, from blows on the outer door. The kitchen-mother crossed herself. It was the sledge-driver. 'I shouldn't have thought you were strong enough to knock like that,' Frank told him.

'How long? How long?'

At the same time the stationmaster, perhaps taking the opportunity to find out what was going on in his house, came in through the front. Probably he was the only person who ever did so. This meant that the whole lot of them — Frank, the children, the kitchen-mother, the stationmaster — had to sit down together for another half-hour. Annie's coat had to be taken off again. She fell asleep again instantly. Tea, cherry jam from the cupboard which could be opened now that the stationmaster had brought his keys. The kitchen-mother suddenly declared that she couldn't bear to be parted from her Dolly, her Daryasha, who resembled so much what she had been like herself as a child. The stationmaster, still wearing his official red cap, lamented his difficulties at the Alexandrovna, where he was besieged by foreign travellers. His clocks all kept strict St Petersburg time, 61 minutes in advance of Central European time and two hours one minute in advance of Greenwich. What was their difficulty?

'You might ask to be transferred to the Donetz Basin,' suggested Ben.

'How old is your boy?'

'Nine,' said Frank.

'Tell him that the Alexandervokzal is the top appointment. There is nothing higher. The state railways have nothing higher to offer me. But it's not his fault, he's young, and besides that, he's motherless.'

'Where's your wife, for that matter?' Frank asked. It turned out that, trusting no-one in Moscow, she had gone back to her village to recruit more waitresses for the spring season. They prepared to go, the sleigh-driver pointing out, for the first time, that the horse was old.

'How old is he exactly?' asked Ben. 'There are regulations, you know, about how old they're allowed to be.' The sleigh-driver said he was a young devil.

'They're all young devils,' said Frank. 'Now I want to get them home to Lipka Street.'

They might have been away several years. The whole household, the house itself, seemed to be laughing and crying. From the carnival – that was what it felt like – only Dunyasha was absent. Almost at once she came to Frank for her internal passport, which was necessary if you were going to make a journey of more than fifteen miles, and had to be handed over to the employer. She wanted to leave, she was no longer happy in the house, where criticisms were being made of her. Frank took it out of the drawer in his study where he kept such things locked away. He felt like a man with a half-healed wound who would do better to leave it alone, for fear of making bad worse. Nellie had sent no message to him by the children, not a word, and he saw it would be best not to think about this, or he might not be able to stand it. His father had always held that the human mind is indefinitely elastic, and that by the very nature of things we were never called upon to undertake more than we could bear. Frank had always felt doubtful about this. During the past winter one of the machine men from the Press had gone by night to a spot a little way out of the Windau station, and lain down on the tracks. This was because his wife had brought her lover to live in their house. But the height of the train's wheelbase meant that it passed right over him, leaving him unhurt, like a drunken peasant. After four trains had passed he got up and took the tram back to his home, and had worked regularly ever since. This left the question of endurance open.

While the rejoicing went on and spread to the yard and, apparently to the yard dog and to the hens, locked up for the winter, Dolly came in wearing her brown uniform from the Ekaterynskaya Gymnasium, and asked him to help her with her homework, since after all, she had to be at school by nine o'clock. She spread out her atlas, ruler, and geography exercise book.

'We're doing the British Isles. We have to mark in the industrial areas and the districts largely given over to keeping sheep.'

'Did you take those with you on the train?' asked Frank.

'Yes. I thought they might come in useful, even if I didn't ever get back to the Ekaterynskaya.'

'It was lonely in the house while you were away, somewhat lonely, anyway.'

'We weren't away for very long.'

'Long enough for me to see what it was going to be like.'

Dolly asked: 'Didn't you know what mother was doing?'

'To tell you the truth, Dolly, no, I didn't.'

'I thought not,' she added rapidly. 'It was hard on her. After all, she'd never had to look after us before, Dunyasha did everything. Annushka wouldn't sit still. Mother asked the attendant for some valerian drops, to calm her down, but he hadn't any. We should have brought some with us, of course, but I didn't do the packing. You shouldn't have expected her to manage by herself. She had to send us back, we weren't a comfort to her. I think you asked too much of her.'

'I don't agree, Dolly. I know my own mind, but so does your mother.'

# 3

Frank's father, Albert Reid, had looked ahead – not quite far enough, perhaps, but to see too clearly in Russia is a mistake, leading to loss of confidence. He was aware that the time was coming when British investors, ironmasters, mill-owners, boiler-makers, engineers, race-horse trainers and governesses would no longer be welcome. Either the Russians would take everything into their own hands or the Germans would, but he thought that the good times would last a while yet. All that had really been needed, when he started out in the 1870s, was a certificate to say that the articles of association of your company were in accordance with British law and another form in St Petersburg to say that your enterprise was advantageous to the interests of the Russian Empire. Besides that, though, you had to have a good digestion, a good head for drink, particularly spirits, a good circulation and an instinct for how much in the way of bribes would be appropriate for the uniformed and for the political police, the clerks from the Ministry of Direct Import, Commerce and Industry, and the technical and sanitary inspectors, to get anything at all. These bribes, too, must be called gifts, and with that word you began your study of the Russian language. All the other formalities – sending the balance sheets, for example, to the central government and the local Court of Exchequer – were just paperwork, which he'd done himself, with his wife's help, by lamplight, in the old wooden house on the works site in the Rogoznkaya. Like the Russian nobility and the Russian merchants, foreign businesses were given ranks, according to their capital and the amount of fuel (soft coal, birchbark, anthracite, oil) that their factory consumed. Reid's (Printing Machinery) was of moderate rank. Frank's father and mother were the only partners. Both of them had come from long families, that was why Bert had been sent out in the first place to make a living in Russia, but they only had the one son. Frank was sent over to England once or twice as a boy, to stay with his relatives in Salford. He enjoyed himself in Salford because, given half a chance, he enjoyed himself anywhere. When he was eighteen he went back for much longer, to train in mechanical engineering and printing, first at Loughborough Polytechnic, then for his apprenticeship with Croppers of Nottingham.

It was while he was at Croppers, doing quite reasonably well, and playing football for the first time in his life, that his father wrote to him to say that, as a kind of subsidiary to the business, he was going to start his own printing press, quite near the centre of Moscow, in Seraphim Street. There was nothing legal at the moment against foreigners buying property, as long as it wasn't in Turkestan or the Caucasus or anywhere where they were likely to strike oil, and he thought the place could be got fairly cheap. He'd start with hand presses only, jobbing machines, and see how they went along. It was an old warehouse, this place, and there was room to expand. Even though the deal wasn't concluded yet, the men were already calling it Reidka's — dear little Reids.

There was a photograph enclosed of Seraphim Street, looking like most of Moscow's side-streets, almost past repair, blank, narrow, patched and peeling, with children crowded around a horse and cart selling something unidentifiable. Above was a white sky with vast, even whiter clouds. The shop-signs made Frank feel homesick. Perlov's tea-bricks, Kapral cigarettes 20 for 5 kopeks, and a kabak with a name that looked like Markel's Bar.

His father usually gave the date Russian style, thirteen days earlier than the date in Nottingham, so that there was some adjustment to be done, but it must have been in March that year that there was mention of Selwyn Crane, who'd been taken on, not at the works, but to do the accounting at Reidka's. A few weeks later it seemed that Crane was becoming very religious. 'I've no objection to that, though on the whole I think religion is of more use to a woman than a man, as it leads to content with one's lot.' In the next letter, Bert doubted whether 'religious' was quite the right word. 'Spiritual' would be better. 'Crane has now proclaimed himself a vegetarian, which I do not think is enjoined anywhere in the Bible, and he tells me he's several times been in quite lengthy conversations with Count Tolstoy. Tolstoy is a very great man, Frank,' he continued. 'Fortunately, though, one doesn't have to judge of great men by the oddities of their disciples. The truth is, though, that Crane has a knack with figures and has been up to now a pretty fair man of business – he came to me from the Anglo-Russian Bank. I asked him whether it was not rather surprising that he should have saved a reasonable sum of money, as I fancy he has done – he is not a married man – and continues to live off the said sum and the salary I pay him, while giving it out as his opinion that buying or selling of any kind or description is a sin against mankind. It's rather, he said, that wealth shouldn't be used for the benefit of individuals. Then, you consider me a wrong doer, Crane, I said, determined to treat the whole matter in a spirit of joke, the next thing will be that you'll refuse to shake me, your employer, by the hand. I thought I'd caught him there, but what he did was to kiss me, first on one cheek and then on the other – a Russ habit, as you well know, but this was on the shop floor, Frank, not even in the counting house.'

His father, however, had no hesitation about the chief

compositor he'd engaged, a capital fellow, a very steady worker, it would take a revolution to dislodge Yacob Tvyordov. Frank thought, when the time comes, I'll see whether I want these people or not. I'll make up my own mind when it comes to it.

In 1900 he transferred himself to Hoe's of Norbury to get experience with more up-to-date machines. It was in Norbury that he met Nellie Cooper. She lived with her brother Charles, who was a solicitor's clerk, and his wife Grace, at 62 Longfellow Road. It was a nice, substantial house, two entrance doors, the inner one with a stained glass panel, good new glass in art shades from Lowndes and Drury, representing the Delectable Mountains from the Pilgrim's Progress, dining room and kitchen downstairs in the basement, sitting room opening on to a flight of green-painted iron steps which led into the garden, a bit of fencing to screen off the vegetables, three bedrooms on the first floor, one of them spare as Charles and Grace didn't have any children. Frank had a room in a boarding house where, the landlady, probably unintentionally, as it seemed to him, was gradually starving him to death. He joined (as he had done in Manchester and Nottingham) the local choral society. At refreshment time (they were rehearsing, perhaps overrehearsing, *Hiawatha*) he had to excuse himself to Nellie, who was helping to serve out, for taking more than one fish paste roll. Nellie asked him what his job was, whether he had to heave things about in the open air and couldn't help getting up an appetite. Then, without listening very attentively to his answer, she said she had been teaching for four years and was due to take her qualifying exam for the certificate.

'I'm twenty-six,' she added, as though it might as well be said now as later.

'Do you like teaching?'

'Not all that much.'

'You oughtn't to go on with it then. You oughtn't to try for the certificate. You ought to train to do what you want to do, even if it's sweeping the streets.'

Nellie laughed. 'I'd like to see my brother's face.'

'Does he worry about you?'

'He's doing all right, anyway. I suppose there's no real need for me to work at all.'

'I don't know why you do it, then.'

'It gets me out of the house, so I'm not under my sister-in-law's feet and she doesn't have to see me all day.'

'Did she say that to you, Miss Cooper?'

'No, she wouldn't say anything like that. She's a sufferer.'

Frank was struck by her way of looking at things. There was a tartness about it, a sharp flavour, not of ill-nature, but of disapproval of life's compromises, including her own. The introduction meant that he was entitled to see her home from the draughty Jubilee Hall where the rehearsals had been called. Nellie had to help put away the Choral Society's crockery. Then she came back in her coat, with her shoes in a water-proof bag. Frank, to establish his claim, took the bag from her. He always did everything quickly and neatly, without making a business of it.

'If we were in Moscow now it would still be all frozen up,' he said, going down the steps beside her.

'I know,' said Nellie. 'But when you do things at school in geography you know them, but you don't believe them.'

'No, you have to see them for yourself. It makes you want to do that.'

'Were you at school in Russia, then?'

'Yes, I was,' he said.

'Well, if you'd read about Norbury while you were there, tell me honestly, would you have wanted to come and see it?'

'I would,' Frank answered, 'if I had known I was going to be in such good company.'

She ignored this, but Frank felt satisfied. He asked her what she thought of *Hiawatha*. She told him that the composer lived in Croydon, not so far away, and this was supposed to be his favourite among all his pieces. 'He christened his son Hiawatha, you know.'

'But what's your opinion of the music, Miss Cooper?'

'To be honest, I don't care so very much for music. I can hold a part all right, but only as long as I'm with a lot of others. I don't know how I got through my sight-singing test when I came to join the society. I've often wondered about that. Dr Alden, that was the old choirmaster, didn't hardly seem to listen. Perhaps he'd been drinking.'

'Well, but there you are again. Why do you come to rehearsals, if you don't care about them?'

It was the same reason — to get out of the house, to get out of the way of her sister-in-law, who, when Frank met her, seemed harmless enough, but harmlessness, as he knew, could be a very hard thing to bear. When he went to Longfellow Road to call for Nellie, Grace Cooper would fuss over him and ask him whether his landlady was treating him right. She told him to leave his shaving mirror in the bed during the day and if by the evening it was clouded over that meant that the bed was damp, and he had a right to complain about it at the Town Hall. Better take the mirror along with him, to show to the authorities. Frank got the notion that Grace always talked about damp.

Several times he was asked to stay to supper, and they sang hymns afterwards at the piano. Frank realized then that Nellie had told the truth about her voice, and he admired her for telling the truth.

The trouble was that he was still only training. His lodgings and laundry cost him twelve shillings and five-pence a week, and by Saturday he was hard up. 'I know how you're placed,' said Nellie, 'I'll pay my share.'

'I'm not sure I could agree to that,' Frank said.

'You're afraid I'll take out my purse and lay it on the table and rattle it about, getting out the money. Don't get that idea into your head. Just as we go out, before we ever get out of the house, I'll give you something for my half. That way there can't be any awkwardness. It's called Dutch treat, you know. What's that in Russian?'

There was no Russian word for it. 'Students, perhaps,' said Frank, 'I've seen them empty out their pockets at the beginning of the evening and put all the money they've got in the middle of the table.'

'That's not Dutch treat,' said Nellie.

Once he had his training certificates, he had reasonably good prospects to lay before her. He felt that he could assume that she wouldn't be too distressed at leaving her family and friends, still less at getting out of Norbury. If he wanted to go ahead with it, he ought to speak to Charlie, explaining in more detail about the firm and his prospects. He did want to go ahead with it, and after fixing things up with Nellie, he did speak to Charlie. No worry about a ring, because he had brought with him a ring belonging to his mother which his father had bought for her at Ovchini-kof's in Moscow. It was a Russian triple knot, in three different colours of gold, made so that the three circlets were separate but could never be taken apart. They slid and shone together on Nellie's capable finger. At the choral society it was thought pretty, but foreign-looking. 'When your mother gave it you, she must have expected you to find someone,' said Nellie. 'Was she ill?'

'I don't think so, she certainly didn't say so?'

'What were the girls like in Nottingham?'

'I can't remember. Very moderate, I think.'

'I daresay they fancied you because you were tall?'

'They might have done.'

'Did you fall in love with any of them when you were in Manchester, or when you were in Nottingham, and offer them this ring, and get turned down?'

'No Nellie, I didn't.' They were walking in Norbury Park. The air and the trodden earth and grass breathed out moisture. Grace had warned them that they would find it very damp.

'You might have had to take the ring back to Moscow, then, and tell your mother it was no go.' They sat down on a bench, from which an elderly man tactfully got up as they approached.

'Look here Frank, do you know a lot about women?' He was undaunted.

'I think you'll find I know quite enough for the purpose, Nellie.'

There was no need to wait a long time for the wedding. Frank's parents had to arrange to come from Moscow, and it was never easy for them to leave the business, but all his relatives from Salford were singlemindedly devoted to attendance at weddings and funerals, and would let nothing stand in their way. The preparations made Frank resolve never, until he came to be buried, to let himself become an object of attention at any kind of religious ceremony again. He knew, however, that he ought not to grumble. Both Charlie and Grace, who were going, after all, to considerable expense, told him that it would be Nellie's day. He felt deeply tender towards her because of this and because of her practical good sense and the number of lists she was making and the letters which were answered and crossed off yet another list. He was startled when she said: 'I'm doing all this as it should be done, because I owe it to both of us. But I'm not going to be got the better of by Norbury.'

'They wouldn't dare,' Frank said. 'Which of them would?'

'You don't think I'm marrying you, Frank Reid, just to get out of Norbury?'

'I don't put myself as low as that,' he said, 'or you either.'

'I don't just mean the people here,' she went on earnestly, 'I mean all the people we've invited, those cousins of yours from Salford, and those aunts.'

'They're not so bad.'

'People always say that about their aunts,' said Nellie. 'The wedding will bring out the worst in them, you'll see. I'm not a dreamer. I have to look at things quite squarely, as they really are. That's one of the things you like about me. I know it is.'

She had no doubts. Even her curling hair seemed to spring up from her forehead with determination. Frank kissed her, but not in such a way as to interrupt her. She asked him whether he'd given any thought as to what the wedding would be like.

'It's best to take things as they come,' he said.

'Well, I'll tell you what it's going to be like. I'm not talking about the church service. I mean afterwards, when we're back here. We're going to have ham and tongue, cucumber sandwiches, vanilla shape and honeycomb mould, nuts, port wine and Madeira. The port wine will be a bit much for Charlie and after a bit it'll be too much for the lot of them, and they'll all take some, because teetotallers always say that port doesn't count, and the older ones, they'll draw together a bit and lower their voices and say to each other, she doesn't know what she's in for. She's twenty-six and he's the first boy she's ever been out with seriously. He's a decent sort, you can see that, so they won't have been up to anything yet, and she hasn't any idea what she's in for.'

'I was hoping they'd have confidence in me,' said Frank, 'they've no reason not to.'

'Oh, they won't have anything against you personally. But they have to make out that it's a tremendous thing – the only thing that ever happens to a woman, really, bar having children, and change of life, and dying. That's how they see things in Norbury. There's a certain expression they have, I've noticed it so often. They'll say that if they'd known what it was going to be like nothing would have dragged them to the altar.'

Frank felt rather at a loss. He kissed her again and said, 'Don't be discouraged.' She remained rigid.

'What does it matter what all these people think, Nellie? If you're really right, we ought to pity them.'

Nellie shook her head like a terrier.

'I'm not going to be got the better of. They may not know it, they won't know it, but I'm not going to.'

It was a brilliant day, a moment when a Norbury's dampness justified itself in bright green grass, clipped green hedges, alert sparrows, stained glass washed to the brilliance of jewels, barometers waiting to be tapped. They were alone in the house. Nellie said: 'Would you like to see my things? I mean the things I'm going to wear for the wedding. Not the dress, they'll bring that later. It's not lucky to have it in the house for too long.'

'Yes, of course I would, if you feel like showing them to me.'

'Do you believe in luck?'

'You've asked me that before, Nellie. I told you, I used to believe it was for other people.'

They went up past the half-landing and into a bedroom almost entirely filled by the wardrobe and various pieces of furniture which looked as though they'd come to rest there from other rooms in the house. The morning sunlight, streaming through the one window caught the wardrobe's bright bevelled glass. On the white bed some white draper's goods were laid out, turning out to be a petticoat, a chemise, drawers and corsets. These last Nellie picked up and threw on the ground.

'I'm not wearing these. I've given up wearing them. From now on I'm going to go unbraced, like Arts and Crafts women.'

'Well, it's always beaten me how women can stand them,' said Frank.

'Don't think I'm going to pay for them, though. They can go back to Gage's.'

'Why not?'

'They make ridges on your flesh, you know, even with a patent fastener. You'll find I don't have any ridges.'

She began to undress. 'I'm twenty-six.'

'You keep telling me that, Nellie.'

'All the same, even at my age, when I've got these things off I'm not sure what to do next.'

It was a moment's loss of confidence, which Frank knew he mustn't allow. Under his hands her solid partly naked body was damp with effort. She was recklessly dragging off something or other whose fastenings seemed to defy her. Her voice was muffled. 'Go on Frank. I'm not going to let them stand about knowing more than I do. I won't be got the better of.'

# 4

The young Reids did not go straight to Moscow. One of the things that Frank's father had told him at the Norbury wedding was that he'd better have a look at what they were doing in Germany, and so for three years he worked with Hirschfeld's printing machinery in Frankfurt. Dolly was born there, and so was Ben. Then came the miscarriage. It was summertime, the hot, landlocked German summer. They were living in the suburbs, and in those days there were still barrel organs playing in the streets. From the pavement below their room an organ repeated the same tune *Schön wie ein engel*. Again and again it tore into the sentimental music with steel teeth. Nellie lay flat on her back, losing blood, hoping to save the baby. She told Frank to throw some money out of the window to the organ-man to bring them luck, but they had no luck that day.

In the winter of 1905 Bert Reid died in Moscow — not in the uprisings, although that was a year of strikes and violence, almost a revolution against the Russian war with Japan. The German and English papers showed pictures of the streets barricaded with wrecked trams. The electricity had been cut off and the snowy, tomb-like barricades were lit by kerosene flares. Five batteries of artillery arrived to shell the factories in the Presnya and the Rogoznkaya where the men held out. Then they pumped in water through the gaps with equipment borrowed from Moscow's fire services. The water turned to ice on impact. When the strikers came out to try to escape back to their villages, the soldiers overturned their sledges and scattered their possessions in the snow. The assembly plant was taken over and the Reids moved to the nearest hotel, Sovastyanov's. There, after a week during which he had no occupation, since the army wouldn't let him on to his own site, Bert complained of heart pains. These pains were the symptoms of bacterial endocarditis. Pieces of inflamed tissue were making their way from the walls of the heart into the bloodstream. The Greek doctor who was called in — their usual doctor, a German, had left for Berlin when the light and water in his surgery was cut off — had nothing to prescribe except rest and valerian drops and warm water. He told Mrs Reid that in his opinion her husband's heart had given way from grief at the sad happenings in St Petersburg and Moscow. But Dr Weiss, if he had been there, though he might have diagnosed more accurately, would not have been able to save Bert.

Mrs Reid, perhaps, really did die of grief. She collapsed

in the study of the Anglican chaplaincy, where she had gone to see about the funeral arrangements. Summoned by cables, Frank arrived at the Alexander station with Nellie and the two children, who wanted to start playing immediately in the deep snow. He remembered – though she had left no will and indeed had nothing of her own – that she had expressed a wish to be buried in Salford. All that had to be put in hand, and he had to find somewhere to live. The wooden family house on the site had been half burned down and then swamped with water. Without much difficulty he took a lease on 22 Lipka Street. Some of the men got together to help him rescue what furniture they could. The piano, oddly enough, his mother's Bechstein, came out undamaged from the ordeal by fire and ice. Everything else he got from Muir and Merrilees, which had remained open during what the manager called the disturbances, its dark blue flag with the golden M&M flying frozen above the shop's façade.

It wasn't a time for risk-taking, because Frank was determined that Nellie shouldn't have to worry about money. A look through the books showed that the import and assembly business would have to be wound down, or better still, sold as it stood. That was a pity, because Reid's main suppliers, Hoe's of the Borough Road in south east London, were as reliable as the day and the night. The trouble seemed to have been two things which

Frank hadn't known anything about. In the first place, although his father had got his letters, giving him some idea of the German competition, he hadn't acted on the advice, or had acted on it eccentrically. He'd set his heart on expansion, and, worst still, become fascinated by the idea of the Mammoth Press which Hoe's were putting into production for Lloyds Weekly News at a cost of eighteen thousand pounds. Another Mammoth, not for any definite customer, but most unwisely ordered on spec, had been delivered to the site, and was lying prone under tarpaulin, colossal, unassembled, unpaid for, looking, as it lay under many inches of snow against the pale green sky, like an ominous relic of the past rather than the machinery of the future. By Bert Reid's bedside when he died, among the letters he was drafting to the Ministry of Interior to plead for those of his people, his 'hands', who had been arrested, was an illustrated booklet from Hoe's describing, in heroic terms, the Mammoth. Now, with the sheds, the plant and the site itself, it must find, even in its dismembered state, a purchaser, probably one of the merchants of the second grade, with whose sons Frank had gone to school. Once it was gone, he could strike a balance, and concentrate on Reidka's.

Frank's affection for Moscow came over him at odd and inappropriate times and in undistinguished places. Dear, slovenly, mother Moscow, bemused with the bells of its four times forty churches, indifferently sheltering factories, whore-houses and golden domes, impeded by Greeks and Persians and bewildered villagers and seminarists straying on to the tramlines, centred on its holy citadel, but reaching outwards with a frowsty leap across the boulevards to the circle of workers' dormitories and railheads, where the monasteries still prayed, and at last to a circle of pig-sties, cabbage-patches, earth roads, earth closets, where Moscow sank back, seemingly with relief, into a village.

Nellie, too, very much preferred Moscow to Germany. She enjoyed putting 22 Lipka Street in order. The village habits of the great manufacturing city didn't disconcert her at all. She was at home there, it seemed to Frank. This threw a new light on her hostility to Norbury, which had been neither town nor country.

# 5

They had had to move to Moscow in the dead of winter, and as they came out of the Alexander station the whole Tverskaya seemed to be drifting with smoke and steam, everyone, men and women alike, rolling and smoking their own cigarettes, their breath condensing heavily in the frost, like cattle in a pen. Selwyn had met them, anxious for their welfare and unmistakeably grieving, to be forgiven everything for his sincerity. What had to be forgiven was his inability to help in any way with the children, the porters and the luggage, not so much through incompetence as inability to grasp the kind of thing that might be needed. Frank had met him before on short trips to see his parents in Moscow, Nellie not at all. 'How do you do, Mr Crane. This is Dolly, our eldest. This is Ben.' Selwyn bent down towards them, wrapped as they were like bundles against the cold.

'Both of them bereaved!'

'They've never met their grandparents, so they're hardly likely to miss them,' said Nellie. 'Perhaps you'd help Frank to check the items.'

At that first meeting, she told Frank, she'd thought that Mr Crane was only elevenpence in the shilling. But Selwyn, though he would probably have been at a loss in Frankfurt, managed well enough in Moscow. He didn't oppose his will to the powerful slow-moving muddle around him. What he did not like, or could not change, he guilelessly avoided. The current of history carried him gently with it.

Before his first visit to Reidka's Frank asked Selwyn to sit down with him and give him an accurate idea of what he'd find when he got there. Selwyn began, as his nature was, with reassurance. 'Of course, your chief compositor will be there, Yacob Tvyordov will be there, as always.'

'What happened to him last year? Wasn't he out on strike with the others?'

'He is the Union Treasurer, and he was out for six days. I believe those are the only six days he's ever missed.'

'Where did my father find him?'

'He came from the Flying Swan Press when it closed down. They only did hand-printing, of course.'

'And Tvyordov?'

'Only hand-printing.'

'How old is he?'

'I don't know. We've got his particulars, I suppose. Some people are ageless, Frank.'

'What about the overseer?'

Selwyn never liked to speak ill of another human being. He hesitated.

'Korobyev. Well, it's his business, of course, to collect the fines for mistakes, spoiled work, laziness, drunkenness, absence and so on. An unenviable task, Frank! But there it is, the Printer's Union agreed to the scale of fines, and we keep to the agreed scales. But since your father died, I fear Korobyev may have instituted a collection of his own whenever he feels the need for ready money.'

'Who does he collect from?'

'Well, perhaps from anyone who is not quite strong enough to object. Perhaps from Agafya, our tea-woman, perhaps from Anyuta, our cleaning-woman. Perhaps a few kopeks from the errand boys.'

'Have you spoken to him about it?'

'Your father may have told you that I don't believe in direct resistance to evil. The only way is to put it to shame, to put it to flight, by good example.'

Frank thanked him, went to the press, shook hands with the entire staff, and called a general meeting to discuss the conduct of the overseer. This meant the three hand-compositors and their two apprentices, the pressmen, the readers, the three machine-men, the putting-on and taking-off boys, the gatherers, the folders, the deliverers, the storekeeper, the warehouseman who also entered the work in the account books and checked deliveries, the paper-wetting boys, the errand-boys, the doorman and Agafya and her assistant Anyuta. There was only one place where there was room to address them all at the same time and that was the shed which served both as the paper warehouse and the tea-kitchen. Once they were assembled the men complained that the boys, some of whom were only just fourteen, were incompetent to judge the question, and they were sent home. This cleared a good deal of space. Meantime Korobyev had not arrived, he had not been in at all that day, and was feeling faint.

'Well, we'll proceed without him,' said Frank, taking up his stand on the tea-counter. 'I'm speaking to you, not as a stranger, because as you know, I'm a child of Moscow, but as a stranger to this press which was my father's last enterprise.' Some crossed themselves. 'Because he died, I have come back to you. I think I may say that during my time in England and Germany I've learnt the business pretty thoroughly. Tonight we have to decide between ourselves what is meant at Reid's Press by fair dealing.'

It was the shortest meeting that Frank had ever attended. It appeared that there was no one in the room who did not want to get rid of their overseer. Korobyev did not insist on working out his time, or accept Frank's invitation to explain himself. All he asked for was his internal passport, which allowed him to travel more than fifteen miles from his place of birth, and which an employer, if he thought fit, could refuse to give back. Frank gave it back. As Korobyev left the building, the compositors hammered him out by knocking their sticks against their cases. The battering sound seemed to excite itself and to work itself into a metallic frenzy, splintering the ears. The din stopped as suddenly as it had begun, and outside, at the tram-stop, Korobyev could be heard shouting: 'Listen to me! Let everyone hear what has been done to the father of a family!'

Suddenly Agafya, her head covered with a white handkerchief, went down on her knees before Frank and implored him to have mercy on Korobyev.

'That's all rubbish, Agafya. He was taking forty-seven kopeks a week off your wages.'

'I'm on my knees to you, Frank Albertovich, sir.'

'Yes, I see you.'

'You heard him say he's the father of a family.'

'It's a disgrace if he is,' said Frank. 'He's not married.'

Agafya, satisfied with the dramatic effect she had made, returned, like an old sentry to his post, to her samovars and to her campaign, in which no settlement seemed possible, with the storekeeper, over the issue of tea. The tea came, not in leaf form, but in tablets. These were charged as Consumables, but Frank thought they might just as well go down under Maintenance Materials. Forbidden to smoke, everyone at the Press was impelled to drink black tea not only at the stated hours, but if they could, all day.

From that morning Frank took on the job of overseer himself, or you might say there was no overseer at Reidka's, only a manager who worked rather harder than most. Even so, the change would not have been possible without Tvyordov.

This man was the only compositor to be employed year in year out, on a weekly wage. The other three were on piece work. He had a broad, placid face, and the back of his head, covered with short greying stubble, gave the same reassuring impression as the front. Work started at Reidka's at seven, and at one minute to seven he was in the composing room. It took him a minute exactly to get his setting rule, bodkin, composing-stick and galley out of the locked cupboard where they were kept. These were his own, and he lent them to no one. Tvyordov did not take any tea at this time. He put on a clean white apron which hung from a hook by the side of his frame, and a pair of slippers which he brought with him in a leather bag. Then he stepped into his frame and put his German silver watch on the lower bar of the upper case into a clip of his own construction, which fitted it exactly. The watch had a second hand, or sweep. Tvyordov spent no time in distributing the type from the reserves of the thirty-five letters and fifteen punctuation marks, that had always been done the night before, but started straight away on his copy, memorized the first few phrases, filled his composing stick, adjusted the spaces and took a sounding from his watch to see how long this had taken and to set his standard for the day. This was not an absolute measure. It depended on the weather, the copy, the proportion of foreign words, but never on Tvyordov himself. If at any point later on in the day he found that he had pushed down his last space a few seconds too early he would wait, motionless and untroubled, then shift his setting rule down at the watch's precise tick. When the stick was lifted into the galley he grasped the letters lightly as though they were a solid piece of metal. This was difficult, the apprentices trying it were often reduced to tears, but during the past four hundred years no easier way had apparently been discovered of doing it. In this way he could set one thousand five hundred letters and spaces in an hour.

At three minutes to ten Tvyordov took a cup of tea, which necessitated going down to the canteen, and went to the washroom. This was one of the breaks made compulsory by the unions during the brief period after the government had been frightened by the disturbances, when they were allowed to negotiate. It was said that when Tvyordov had taken to the streets he had been wounded, or damaged in some way. A great many shots had hit people for whom they were not intended. There was certainly no sign of any damage now.

After his tea, at ten o'clock, Tvyordov took his lunch, and at eleven he lifted his type again, his head and body sympathetic to the ticking watch. At twelve he went home for his dinner, and in the afternoons was less silent, but only marginally. There was something indescribably soothing in the proceedings of Tvyordov. There was nothing mechanical about them. There were many minute variations, for instance in the way he washed the type free of dirt and, while it was still just moist enough to stick together, lifted a small amount on to his brass slip, resting it against the broad middle finger of his left hand. No one could tell why these variations occurred. Perhaps Tvyordov was amusing himself. What would he consider amusing? On Saturday nights, when Agafya was seeing to the oil-lamp in front of the composing-room's ikon, Tvyordov wound up the office clock. On his way home, on Saturdays only, he stopped for five minutes exactly at Markel's Bar for a measure of vodka. On Monday mornings he arrived thirty seconds earlier than usual, to clean the clock glass for the week. No one else was trusted to do that.

There was no mystery about Tvyordov's attitude to the machine-room. Linotype, he felt, was not worthy of a serious man's carefully measured time. It was only fit for slipshod work at great speed. To make corrections you had to reset the whole line, therefore you had orders not to do it. The metal used was a wretchedly soft alloy.

Monotype, after some consideration, he tolerated. The machine was small and ingenious, and the letters danced out as they were cast from the hot metal, separate and alive. They weren't as hard as real founder's type, still they would take a good many impressions, and they could be used for corrections in the compositors' room. When, or even whether, Tvyordov had been asked for his views was not known, but Reidka's did monotype, and no linotype.

Probably the very fact that Tvyordov was known to work there had attracted commissions to Reidka's. There was plenty of small work, for which hand-setting was still necessary. Reidka's printed parcel labels, auctioneers' catalogues, handbills of rewards for information leading to the arrest of thieves and murderers, tradesmen's cards, club cards, bill heads, bottle wrappers, doctors' certificates, good quality writing paper, concert programmes, tickets, time sheets, visiting cards, circulars of debts, posters (in three colours, if wanted, at a third more per 100). Frank also accepted leaflets and some magazines and school books, but no newspaper work, and no poetry. There was one exception here, Selwyn's poems, entitled *Birch Tree Thoughts*, which would soon be ready for the press, and where could they be printed but Reidka's? *Birch Tree Thoughts* was at the censor now, and since all poetry was suspect, would perhaps be more carefully read there than it ever would be again. But Frank didn't expect requests for printing from revolutionaries or politicals. These people seemed to be able to produce, almost at will, the illegal manifestos and threats that livened the bloodstream of the city. Frank wondered, and even sometimes tried to calculate, how many printing presses were hidden away in students' garrets and cellars, in cowsheds, bath houses and backyard pissoirs, hen coops, cabbage-patches, potato-stacks — small hand-presses, Albions probably, printing on one side only, spirited away to another address at the hint of danger. He imagined the dissidents, on Moscow's a hundred and forty days a year of frost, warming the ink to deliver one more warning. Printer's ink freezes readily.

When he judged he had the feel of things at Reidka's, Frank made a call on all the other shops and offices in Seraphim Street. There was a regulation imposing tax on new businesses according to the amount of nuisance they caused to the neighbours. To circumvent this, Frank suggested that he should contribute to the street's welfare by paying the wages of a nightwatchman, to patrol the street up to the point where it joined the Vavarkaya. There was a room over Markel's Bar where he could sleep during the day.

'But Frank, there's a hint of bribery here,' said Selwyn.

'Put the wages down to overheads,' Frank told him.

# 6

In 1911, then, Dolly was eight, and wore a sailor suit with a pleated skirt, banded with rows of white. Ben was seven, and also wore a sailor suit, with buttoned boots. Both of them had sailor hats made for them at Muirka's, bearing the name of a British ship, HMS *Tiger*. Dolly was preparing for her entrance to the Gymnasium. She was almost a schoolgirl, but was not afraid to grow older, because she knew that there was in store for her some particular greatness. Towards autumn, Annushka was born. She was delivered by the midwife, the babka. Dr Weiss, long since back in Moscow, came in later, competent, carbolic-scented, eager to talk to Frank about his personal investments. When he had gone, the babka sprinkled Nellie and the baby with holy water and brought tea brewed from raspberry leaves. She had already told Frank to buy a small gold cross and chain, and this was put round Annushka's neck, to remain there for the rest of her life. Dolly and Ben, who had no gold crosses, demanded them.

'Shall I get them?' he asked Nellie anxiously. She was

a woman and had the heavy end of the whole business to carry. She answered that he'd better, if he didn't want to be plagued. This struck him as not really fitting the case. Dolly never plagued, it was her habit to ask for things only once.

Charlie wrote regularly, to Frank rather than to Nellie, who was much less likely to answer. He gave a good many details about his health, about the funeral of King Edward VII, and about the Choral Society's monthly concerts, regularly enclosing the programmes. When Annushka was born he wrote at length, enclosing a five-pound note. His letter went on.

You say that the situation is uncertain in Russia and that you believe you ought to be ready to pull up stakes if necessary, but that you must not grumble at that, well, Frank, I would say that at this moment you must be the better off of the two of us − it continues to be a bad winter here, a black frost last night, and I've been told by several acquaintances here that in their houses the contents of the chamber-pots froze, which I believe is very rarely recorded in the South of England, cap that if you can. Then there's the political aspect. Whereas from what you say you have a passable set of workpeople at the Press and a steady foreman, England is now a place of nothing but trouble and strife, which they call popular agitation. We have now eight hundred miners on strike, and if you can tell me how Old England is to be kept running without coal, and how coal can be spirited out of the ground without miners, then I'm not the only one who would be obliged to you. Then the railwaymen are out again, there are troops standing by this time, very different from twenty years ago. You will ask me, are not their grievances very real? Well, what will you say to this, the Printers, too, not only going on strike as far as their daily work is concerned but producing their own sheet, which is dignified by the name of a newspaper. Yes, I am being asked to read with my second cup of tea, instead of my *Daily Mail*, this revolutionary sheet, for I consider it no less. When all this began, *The Times* said that 'the public must be prepared for a conflict between Labour and Capital, or between employers and employed, upon a scale such as has never occurred before,' or it may have been 'such a scale as', I have not the exact words in front of me.

Nellie said that it was quite enough if one person in the household read Charlie's letters. 'He used to talk like that, too. You can't have forgotten that.'

'I suppose he's got time on his hands since poor Grace died,' Frank said. 'His letters do seem to be longer. Well, he sends his love.'

'We don't know him,' said Dolly. 'We don't know our Uncle.'

'I'll send him a message in general terms from the lot of you.'

'You can borrow my Blackbird, if you like,' said Ben. This was his new fountain pen, which troubled him. It was guaranteed not to leak, but writers and school-children knew better. Ben wished to be relieved of the responsibility of the Blackbird, without losing his own dignity.

To Selwyn also Frank had made it clear that he might have to sell Reidka's, and take his family home, in the next few years or so. Opinion in the British community was divided. The British consul, who was only in Category 3, had no opinion to give. Frank thought the chances of having to leave Russia were about fifty-fifty, but wanted to know how Selwyn would be placed. Selwyn replied that he considered himself as a stranger and a pilgrim, who ought always to be ready to move on. There were Tolstoyan settlements, he believed, everywhere in Europe, there was one, for example, at Godalming.

'You have to bring your skills to such places, of course, but that is all that is asked.' He'd bring management accounting, Frank thought, poetry, music, spiritual advice, shoe-making. In summer, he knew, Selwyn wove his own birch-bark shoes before he took to the roads. They just about lasted the trip. He came back through the Sukhareva Market to the north of Moscow, bought himself a pair of leather boots there, and went back to Reidka's.

Long before his death last year Tolstoy had fallen hopelessly out of fashion with thinking Russia, but not with his foreign disciples, and certainly not with Selwyn. What Tolstoy had thought of Selwyn, Frank was not too sure. Selwyn had been welcome at his Moscow house in Dolgo-Khamovnicheski Street, and Frank believed that he had first met Tolstoy at the Korsakov private lunatic asylum which adjoined the property. Tolstoy had forbidden any repairs to the fence, so that the patients could put their hands through gaps and pick the flowers if they felt like it. There were regular concerts at Korsakov's, got up by the innumerable charities of Moscow. Selwyn had a fine tenor voice, a reasonable tenor voice anyway, which was what passed for a fine one in Russia, the land of basses, and — never having been known to refuse an appeal to his kindness — he had given a recital one evening. What he had sung Frank didn't know, but some of the patients in the audience had become restless, and others had fallen asleep. Selwyn, who told the story without a hint of vanity or resentment, had sung on, but afterwards, since there was no applause, he had taken the opportunity to apologize to Tolstoy, who was sitting in one of the back rows. At the time Tolstoy made no reply, but a few days later he had said: 'I find you have done well. To be bored is the ordinary sensation of most of us at a concert of this kind. But to these unfortunates it is a luxury to have an ordinary sensation.'

'Are you going to sing for them again?' Frank had asked. 'Of course, if Dr Korsakov invites me. But he thinks the experience shouldn't be repeated too often.'

Frank didn't in any way contest the greatness of Lev Nicolaevich, but his hopes for the immediate future of Russia lay with the Premier, Piotr Stolypin. Something about Stolypin's neatness, quietness and correctness, his ability to keep his head, his refusal, when Rasputin tried to hypnotize him, to be affected in the slightest degree, his decision to accept the premiership even though his enemies had tried to dissuade him from politics by blowing him up in his own house and crippling his young daughter, who had lost both her feet — something about all this suggested that Stolypin might, in Nellie's phrase, not be got the better of. Stolypin asked for ten years in power. He gambled on ten years. By offering government loans to Russia's one hundred and seventy-nine million peasants, so that they could buy their own land, he intended — if he was given ten years — to prevent revolution. Stolypin, however, had, as part of his official duties, to accompany the Tsar to a gala performance at the opera house in Kiev. He was in disgrace with the Imperial family and so was not invited to the royal box, but given a seat in the stalls. When he stood up in the interval he presented an excellent target to a terrorist agent in the theatre, who had been unwisely hired by the police as a security man. Stolypin was shot through the lungs and liver, and died four days later.

A memorial fund was opened, but foreigners living in Russia were not allowed to contribute. Frank was sorry about this.

'But would you call him a just man?' Selwyn asked anxiously.

'No, not at all, he fixed the elections and he fixed the members of the Duma, but then the Duma wasn't designed to work in the first place. He didn't make any profits for himself, though, and he saw there was a way for the country to survive without a revolution.'

'A man of courage.'

'Certainly, or he wouldn't have stood up in the theatre.'

Stolypin had asked for ten years, and had been allowed five. In the September of 1911 he was lying in state in an open coffin in Petersburg, just at the time when Nellie felt recovered enough after the birth of Annie to get up and go out a little. She leaned heavily on Frank's arm. They walked a short distance.

'How does it feel being a mother of three?' he asked, not able to contain his love and pride for the new child. 'It'll take up all my time,' Nellie said. 'Still, it took up all my time when I only had Dolly.' 'I hoped Dunyasha would be useful to you. That's all she's supposed to be doing, being of use to you.' 'That Dunyasha!' said Nellie.

They took a taxi to a café on the edge of the Alexander Gardens. There was not a breath of wind, and under the glowing white sky tinged with pink from the horizon which seemed to fume with a warning of frost, the scant leaves were hanging motionless from the lime trees. The waiters who had to serve the tables outside the café were wearing their overcoats over their long aprons. It was the first sting of autumn. In two weeks the statues in the gardens would be wrapped in straw against the cold, all doors would be shut and all windows would be impenetrably sealed up until next spring.

# 7

These sudden decisions of Nellie's — but Frank could really only remember one, in her bedroom in Longfellow Road, that hot afternoon, with just enough breeze, after Frank had drawn the blinds, to make the tassel at the end of the blindcord tap against the window. And she'd accounted to him then for what she felt. In the two years since Annushka was born, had she grown unaccountable?

At first it seemed to him that Nellie must be coming back, and he wired to all the railway stations between Mozhaisk and Berlin. After that he wired to Charlie every six hours. After three days Charlie wired back — Nellie not here, but guaranteed safe and well. Then, as though offering a respectable substitute, he added, shall be coming to Moscow myself shortly. In the confusion, which rapidly became the monotony, of loss it was something to have a fixed point when things must change or be changed, if only by the arrival of Charlie. That was not quite the same thing as wanting him to come, but it meant that Frank had to make arrangements and give instructions, two ways of bringing time to order.

How could Nellie be safe and well without them, the four of them? He wrote to her by every morning post.

'If you want proper envelopes and paper, they're in the right-hand drawer of my desk,' he said to Dolly.

'I know they are.'

'It's locked, but you've only got to ask me.'

'I know.'

'In case you want to write to Mother.'

'Do you mean to ask her why she went away, or to ask her when she's coming back?'

'You don't need to ask either.'

'I shan't need the paper,' said Dolly, 'because I don't think I ought to write. I can only write properly in Russian, in any case.'

'Why not, Dolly? Surely you don't think she did the wrong thing?'

'I don't know whether she did or not. The mistake she probably made was getting married in the first place.'

'Is that what you're going to put in your letter?'

'I told you it would be better if I didn't write one.'

Obviously for a few days at least, perhaps for a few weeks, something would have to be done by way of looking after the children. Annushka had been removed from him, and by her own consent was totally under the doting protection of the cook and kitchen-maid, but he needed help with Ben, and still more with Dolly. With an impulse to avoid the English chaplaincy and the English community for as long as possible, Frank thought of the Kuriatins. Their home was always open to him.

Arkady Kuriatin was a merchant of the second grade. The dues he paid weren't high enough to allow him to export; all his trade was within the Russian empire. He dealt in timber, wood pulp and paper, and Frank had done business with him for some time. Arkady had children – how many, Frank couldn't say, because extra ones, perhaps nephews and nieces, perhaps waifs, or even hostages, seemed to come and go. His wife, Matryona Osipovna, was always at home. Frank had heard her say, 'What is there better outside than in?' Nellie had always admitted Mrs Kuriatin's kindness, but couldn't be doing with her. It was true that she had recommended Nellie to be sure that Dolly and Annushka always had their eyes washed out with their own urine, as this would preserve their bright glances.

Kuriatin had no telephone. Like most of the second-grade merchants he maintained an elaborate pretence, which, however, was a reassurance as well as a pretence, of keeping up the old ways. Sometimes he would indulge himself with the latest improvement. He had a motor-car, a 6-cylinder 50 horse-power Wolseley, of which he was proud, for there were only fifteen hundred cars or so in Moscow. But there was no electric light in his house, and you could not telephone him there.

Fortunately, he chose to live in an unpretentious street
– though the house was large – not far from the Press,
and Frank was able to go round there in the middle of
the morning. He knocked at the outer street door,
although he was perfectly well aware that unless it was
a special occasion, and the Kuriatins were giving a dinner
there would be no one in the front rooms at all. He
waited, and, as he expected, a ferocious looking servant
in a peasant smock appeared round the side of the house,
with the air of a gaoler paid to discourage charitable
visitors. He could not pretend not to recognize Frank,
but shouted, as though to the deaf, the master was
away.

'I'll see Mrs Kuriatin,' said Frank.

To the right, as you went in, was a vast salon, the
shutters closed, the chandeliers wrapped in canvas, the
furniture hidden like corpses under white cotton
shrouds, the whole floor covered for protection with
spread-out sheets of the *Trade Messenger*. On the left the
door was shut, but Frank knew it was the dining room.
Here, when Kuriatin played host, the table clinked and
clashed with imported silver and glass and the fierce
servants were forced out of their smocks and felt boots
and into black coats, shoes, and white gloves. The minor
gentlefolk who had accepted the Kuriatins' hospitality
were not likely ever to invite them in return, but Kuriatin
seemed smilingly to relish this impoliteness. As soon as

the guests had gone, the family migrated to where they really lived, children, servants, dependents and relations on top of one another, in a couple of low-ceilinged, smoky rooms at the very back of the house.

Mrs Kuriatin, who had been lying on a shabby ottoman, flung down her cigarette and heaved herself towards him.

'Ah, Frank Albertovich, if you had come yesterday, when I was feeling poorly, I should not have been able to receive you.'

'Let's be glad that didn't happen, Matryona Osipovna.'

A number of young children were milling about, the tribe of Kuriatin, all of them well-grown, but broad, rather than tall, as though they had adapted themselves to the shape of the room where they spent so much of their time. Two very old women who nodded appeasingly were probably poor relations. One woman he knew – she was the wife of one of Kuriatin's partners, or rather accomplices, in the timber business; the other, in black silk, he didn't know.

'This is my sister, Varya,' cried Mrs Kuriatin. 'Her husband couldn't accompany her, he died not long ago.' Frank took the sister's hand. It was difficult not to feel that he was on a visit to a harem. The air was thick with the smell of lamp-oil and cigarettes from the Greek-tended tobacco gardens of the Black Sea. Mrs Kuriatin now varied her sentence of welcome to: 'If you had come yesterday you would not have been able to see me, and I should not have been able to help you in your trouble.'

Frank looked round the crowded room.

'You're among friends here, Frank Albertovich, and my sister and I are as one person. They say, if Vera slips, Varya falls.'

'Well, let's not call it trouble,' said Frank, 'it's only that as a friend, I'm asking you to do something out of friendship.' Mrs Kuriatin was more than ready. He explained that he did not want Dolly ('That angel!' Mrs Kuriatin exclaimed, rather to his surprise) and Ben to have to be at home by themselves after school. He wondered if, perhaps for a few days only, he hoped, they could come to the Kuriatins instead. He would be able to call round and take them away himself when the Press closed at five o'clock.

Mrs Kuriatin and her sister both shook their heads at the idea of a few days. Out of sheer tenderness of heart they liked every emergency to go on as long as possible. But at least the difficult time had started, and a messenger must be sent at once to Dolly's school and to Ben's, so that they could come that very afternoon. Mitya (Mrs Kuriatin's eldest, referred to as though, like the Crown Prince, his movements must be known to everybody) was coming home early this afternoon, because a special present had been sent to him, for Shrove Tuesday. As to the others – she looked round her with an air of doubtful proprietorship – yes, all, or most, would be there to welcome Dolly and Ben.

Frank sincerely thanked her, and asked her, out of civility, what Mitya's present was. It was a tame bear-cub, or perhaps not tamed, sent down from the North. The prices of ordinary brown bear fur, for rugs and coats, had gone down terribly since they had put proper heating into the Trans-Siberian railway. Still, this one's mother had been shot for sport by one of Arkady's business contacts and generously he had ordered them to box up the cub and put it on the train for Moscow. They knew it had arrived alive, they had been notified from the Yaroslavl station. Only of course it must be fetched. The words, spoken in chorus by Mrs Kuriatin and her sister, gave Frank an uneasy sensation.

When he was a boy he had sometimes been to New Year treats, in Moscow and out in the country, where a performing bear was brought in as an entertainment. There was usually an argument with the door keeper and another with the cook when the animal was brought in through the kitchen. It wore a collar and underneath the bright lights, looked drowsy. First it shifted a little from foot to foot, as though to put them down was painful, then it gave, after a good deal of prompting, what was said to be an imitation first of a Cossack dance, then of an old peasant carrying a heavy load and falling down on the ground, then, as it was led out of the room, of an English governess simpering and looking round over her shoulder at the men. The fur under its collar was worn away, perhaps from doing this particular trick so often. Sometimes it was rewarded with an orange, but, as a joke, the bear-man would take the orange away so that everyone could enjoy its disappointment.

Frank had never been much amused by the dancing bear, nor, as far as he could see, was anyone else. This was only a cub, though. When he got back to Reidka's he told Selwyn what he had arranged, largely for the relief of repeating it aloud. At least he can't make it have anything to do with Tolstoy, he thought. But it turned out that at the New Year Lev Nicolaevich had himself taken the part of the performing bear, wearing a skin which had been lined with canvas. According to Selwyn, this enabled him to give a more spiritual turn to the whole occasion.

# 8

The bear-cub at the Kuriatins' was disappointingly small, and its head looked rather large for its body and seemed to weigh it down. The skin was very loose, as though the cub had not quite grown into it. The dense fur, dark, golden and ginger, grew at all angles, except along the spine which was neatly parted, and on the glovelike paws and hind feet. The protruding claws looked as if they were made of metal, and the bear itself was a dangerous toy. Both front and back legs were bent in an inward curve. The total effect was confused and amateurish, openly in need of protection for some time yet. Planting its feet on the ground in a straight line required thought from the bear, and was not always successful. When Mitya Kuriatin hit it with a billiard cue it turned its torpedo-shaped head from side to side and then fell over.

'Is that all it can do?' asked his sister Masha. 'You said it would dance.'

Mitya, humiliated in front of the English guests with whom he had intended to cut a dash, and by the presence

of an animal when at the age of thirteen he would have
so much preferred something mechanical, shouted 'Well
then, music!' Masha went to the pianola, which Kuriatin
had bought in Berlin with the idea that it would save
the trouble of having his children taught to play the
piano. Perhaps rightly, they took very little interest in it,
and although they knew how to start and stop it they
did not know how to change the music rolls. Now when
Masha turned the switch the idiot contrivance began half
way through. Masha flung herself across the brocaded
piano stool and pressed the key down to loudest. The
bear withdrew to the farthest corner of the room. Turning round with a loud scratching of claws on the
floorboards beyond the carpet, it faced all comers.

'It won't dance, it won't do anything, it's imbecile.'

They tried throwing cold water over it. The bear
sneezed and shook itself, then tried to lick up the spark-
ling drops on the surface of its fur.

'It's thirsty,' said Dolly coldly. After glancing at it for
a moment she and Ben stood together in isolation behind
one of the curtains.

'What are you two talking about?' Mitya called out.

'We're saying that you should give it something to
drink.'

'Yes, it's one of God's creatures,' said the treacherous
Masha.

Mitya blundered out of the room, and came back with

a bottle of vodka and a pale blue saucer of fine china with a gilt rim.

'Where did you get those?' asked Dolly.

'From the dining room. It's all laid out for some reception or other.'

'Are you allowed in there?' said Ben.

'My father's in Riga. I'm the master here!' Mitya's face was red with senseless excitement. He poured the vodka into the saucer and, slopping it over, carried it to the bear's far corner. For the first time its mouth opened and its long dark tongue came out. It tilted its head a little and licked the saucer dry. Mitya poured again, and this time screwing its head round the other way, the little animal drank again.

'Dance now,' shouted Mitya.

The bear got on to its hind legs and was as tall, suddenly, as Mitya, who retreated. Losing its perilous balance it held out its paws like small hands and reeled on to the carpet where its claws gave it a better hold, while a gush of urine sprayed across the pattern of red and blue. For some reason one of its ears had turned inside out, showing the lining of paler skin. It rolled over several times while the dark patch spread, then sidled at great speed out of the door. All the children laughed, Dasha and Ben as well, they were all laughing and disgusted together, the laughter had taken possession of them, broke them in half and squeezed the tears out of their eyes.

'It's gone into the dining room.'

Then they were silent and only Mitya went on grossly laughing as they followed clinging to each other to the front of the house and heard a tearing and rending, then a crash like the splintering of ice in the first spring thaw as the bear, and they could see it now reflected in the great mirrors on every wall, lumbered from end to end of the table making havoc among glass and silver, dragging at the bottle of vodka which stood in each place, upending them like ninepins and licking desperately at what was spilled. The service door flew open and the doorman, Sergei, came in, crossed himself, and without a moment's hesitation snatched up a shovel, opened the doors of the white porcelain stove and scooped out a heap of red-hot charcoal which he scattered over the bear. The tablecloth, soaked in spirits, sent up a sheet of flame. The bear screamed, its screams being like that of a human child. Already alight, it tried to protect its face with its front paws. Mitya was still doubled up with laughter when from the passage outside could be heard the roar of Kuriatin, pleased with himself because he had come home early as his wife had implored him. 'Devils, do I have to let myself into my own house?' He was at the door. 'Why is that bear on fire? I'll put it out of its misery. I'll spatter its brains out. I'll spatter the lot of you.'

Frank, quietly removing Dolly and Ben from the

uproar, would have liked to know where Mrs Kuriatin had been all this time and why Sergei, half idiotic as he was, hadn't thrown water at the wretched animal instead of red-hot cinders. This was the only one of his questions that the children could answer. Sergei had known that bears were lovers of water. Water would never have stopped a bear.

'You told us you thought we could go there every day after school,' said Ben, 'as long as we were reasonably quiet.'

'I don't think that now.'

'What will you say?'

'I shall go round to Arkady Kuriatin's office tomorrow and offer to pay for some, not much, of the damage.'

'Will you ask him what happened to the bear?' asked Dolly.

'No.'

'Its face was burning.'

'I shan't ask him.'

At Kuriatin's, absurdly old-fashioned counting-house, almost next door to his home, as though he wanted to keep watch over both at once, Frank was told once again, this time by a clerk, that the master was out. 'I haven't seen him all day, Frank Albertovich.'

The clerks still used pen and ink and were allowed a fixed number of nibs every week. Their calculations were done on an abacus, whose black and white beads clicked at great speed, fell silent, and then started to click again.

'Well, I've something to say to him, but I shan't take long.'

'What am I to say if I'm asked why I admitted you?' said the clerk.

'Say you haven't seen me all day.'

Not long ago Frank had found that the floor of the machine-room at Reidka's needed strengthening, and Kuriatin had agreed to supply the wood for the new joists. Four days before Frank was due to take delivery, he sent a message that he was ill and couldn't discuss business. Two days later he was surprised that Frank didn't know that he'd given up supplying timber as there was no profit in it for an honest man, and the next day he was said to have gone on a pilgrimage. A week later he was back, but sent word that he couldn't see Frank either then or perhaps ever, because of certain misunderstandings between himself and Frank's father. As to the wood, that was in one of the store houses. That very evening, meeting Frank by chance in the steamroom of the Armenian baths, Kuriatin, very much the worse for drink, embraced him tearfully and asked his forgiveness for having been unable to fulfil the order. The next morning he said sharply that he could have made the delivery some time ago if the percentage tax had been paid to the Ministry of Commerce and Industry, and, of course, something allowed for Grisha, Grigory Rasputin, who was certainly in regular receipt of bribes, though never from Kuriatin, who avoided Petersburg and conducted his business in cash. When the cash was put into his hands he went through it minutely to make sure that there were no 1877 notes, or 100 rouble notes issued in 1866. Neither of these were legal tender. Probably he would have rather been paid in poultryfood, or benzine. Finally, Frank had got his timber, only a few hours later than he had actually allowed for. His calculations had not been far out.

Kuriatin's private office was as dark as the rest of the establishment, and not much more comfortable. On seeing Frank, he opened his arms wide. He was wearing a black kaftan from which came a strong, healthy human odour. An unfortunate incident? The children left to themselves? Damage? Broken china, pissed carpet, fire, destruction, twenty-three and a half bottles of the best vodka? Did Frank think his credit wasn't good enough to bear a little loss, a little trifle? Did he think there was some shortage of tablecloths? All that he'd had to do, on returning, was to dismiss Sergei and some of the women servants, give Mitya a beating, hire sledges, tell the guests when they arrived not even to take off their overcoats and galoshes and drive off with the lot of them to Krynkin's Restaurant.

'I was wondering where your wife could have been at

the time,' said Frank. 'I understood that she would be with the children.'

'She was lying down, as all women do. She's terrified of animals, can't stand them in the house.' But why, Kuriatin continued, why did Frank himself not come to his home that evening, no formality, just to share what God provided?

'No thank you, not this evening, Arkady Filippovich.'

'You won't partake of our simple fare?'

Frank knew the invitation wasn't meant to be accepted. It was out of the question for him to come round like that, as a guest on the spur of the moment. Merchants of the second grade did not entertain in such a way. Preparations would have had to be made. Without them, he would have caused almost as much trouble as the bear.

Kuriatin took Frank's arm and escorted him down the bare wooden stairs, both of them, from long practice, avoiding the weak places.

'Why don't you get something done about these stairs?' Frank asked. 'And why don't you let your clerks have a telephone? The Germans will get ahead of you.'

'Why don't you get your wife to come back to you?' shouted Kuriatin, exploding with laughter, as the doorman came out of his cupboard-like room and ushered them, deeply bowing, into the street. For Kuriatin life, like business, was a game, but not a gambling game. On the contrary, it was one in which he had arranged to win, although the rules were peculiar to himself. Knowing that the children had been put at risk in his half-savage household, he had felt Frank's visit as a reproach. But by insulting Frank – of whom he was genuinely fond – he had restored himself to a superior position. It almost compensated him for the loss of his tablecloth, glass and china, to which he had been insanely attached.

# 9

Frank went straight to the English Chaplaincy off the Marosseika, where he should, perhaps, have gone in the first place. Evening tea-time was one of Mrs Graham's visiting hours. He was not afraid of Mrs Graham, or at least not as afraid as some people were. In any case, in taking his predicament to her he was doing her a service. She was a scholar's daughter, brought up in Cambridge, and not reconciled to living in Moscow. Although she hadn't, Frank knew, attended college herself, she might be called a student of a kind, a student of trouble, or rather of other people's troubles.

'Mr Reid?' she called out in her odd, high, lightly drawling voice. 'This is an expected pleasure.'

'You knew I was going to come and ask you something?'

'Of course.'

Restless as a bird of prey which has not caught anything for several days, she nodded him towards the seat next to her. There were no comfortable chairs in the chaplaincy, except in Mr Graham's study.

Mrs Graham was not alone, indeed she rarely was. Opposite her sofa there sat a woman of about her own age, somewhere between forty and fifty, wearing a grey skirt of stout material, a grey blouse that did not quite match it, a grey spencer with pink bits about it somewhere and a felt hat, put on quite straight. The total effect was that of gallantry in the face of odds. She was introduced as Miss Muriel Kinsman. Frank remembered now that he had been told she was coming to Moscow from the depths of the country, where she'd been a governess, and that she had been unjustly dismissed from her employer's estate and, as usual, a collection was being taken up to help her with her fare home. 'Not only does she look like a dismissed governess, but it's clear that she was born looking like one,' Mrs Graham had told him. 'And that I consider unusually hard on her.' Now he shook hands, saying 'It's a pleasure to meet you, Miss Kinsman. I'm only sorry you're not staying longer in Moscow.'

Miss Kinsman fixed him with her great melancholy eyes in her weatherbeaten face. 'I'd stay here willingly if there was anyone who took the least interest in whether I did or not.'

'But you'll be going home to your family?'

She made no answer, and Frank feared he'd been impolite. Bad luck if he was to be reproached for that when in fact he cared amazingly little whether she went home or not.

Mrs Graham said, 'I'm inclined to think sometimes that it's a pity there's such a thing as a postal service. The pain of waiting for letters which don't come very much exceeds the pleasure of getting them when they do. I hope I've said that the right way round. Miss Kinsman hasn't heard from anyone in England for some years.'

'I should like you to call me Muriel, Mrs Graham, even if only once. I should just like to hear that name again.'

'What did they call you out at Vladislavskoe?'

Miss Kinsman explained that although the German governess (who was admittedly younger, or anyway a few years younger, than herself) had always been called Fraülein Trudi, she herself had never been anything but Missy.

'Whatever did that matter?' asked Mrs Graham. 'I shouldn't mind being called Missy.'

'Everything matters when you got out to one of those places. Nothing arrives without your seeing it come out of the forest two versts away, and down the dip, out of the dip, up the road so that by the time it gets to the house, cart or carriage or motor-car or whatever it is, you're sick of it already, so you're driven to brood all day about what's going on in the house itself, and I suppose that gets magnified, every little thing that's said, every bark and shout, every tick and tock. Perhaps one loses one's sense of proportion. Yes, one certainly does.

One incident gets added to another, and it's the sum total of them all that weighs one down.'

The matter of the lost key to the clock. The matter of the lost key to the wine-cooler. The matter of the valerian drops. The matter of the Giant's Stride. The matter of the cigar case. The matter of the pickled cucumber. The matter of the bath house. The matter of the torn photograph . . . she's drifting, thought Frank, and presumably she's come here to drift, for a length of time which would be decisively fixed by Mrs Graham. He felt sorry for her.

'Wasn't it quite what you expected?' he asked.

'There shouldn't be such a state of mind as expectation,' interrupted Mrs Graham. 'One gets too dependent on the future.'

She offered a box of Crimean cigarettes. Frank refused, but not Miss Kinsman, who said, 'I'm afraid I've formed the habit since I came to Russia.'

'So have I,' said Mrs Graham, 'my husband wishes I hadn't. But I smoke the *mahorka*.' Not always, thought Frank, but she did on this occasion, rapidly rolling up the coarse workman's shag in a piece of yellow paper. She lit it and tossed back her head. The cigarette hung from the corner of her mouth, where it looked quite in keeping with her wild grey Cambridge knot of hair, her peasant sarafan worn with a tweed skirt and her bead necklaces. 'Tell!' she cried, puffing.

Miss Kinsman rambled on, in a low voice, not always easy to follow. Although it seemed that some object, always the same one, perhaps the cigar case, perhaps the cucumber, had repeatedly made its appearance in her room and had suggested to her that the whole household was hostile to her and was showing this in petty ways – 'in pranks' Miss Kinsman said – the main trouble had been a noble one, her high concept of education. The Lvovs themselves appeared to take no interest in their children's lessons, that was left to Pavel Borisovich, an unmarried Uncle who was installed in the house, with not much to do except interfere. This Pavel Borisovich had been intended for the College of Pages, but had been sent to school in Berlin, and thought it right to impose an absurdly strict regime on the children. His enthusiasm wouldn't have lasted, of course, nothing did, he just had one craze after another – languages, psychology, gymnastics. It was during his gymnastics mania that he'd got one of the estate carpenters to install a Giant's Stride in the garden after the last hay had been cut. She had thought it her duty to say that it wasn't, in her opinion, a safe piece of apparatus. You stepped out, holding one of the six ropes, into the air and whirled faster, even faster, from one landing-place to another. It was certain to lead to broken bones. But it isn't always a good thing to be in the right.

'It's good, but it's hardly ever safe,' said Mrs Graham.

She was, or probably was, a kind-hearted woman, but she was too sharp, Frank thought. All sharp people, no matter whether they were men or women, were tiring.

The matter of the Giant's Stride. The matter of the Lvov children's timetable. Learning should not be associated with enforcement, but with freedom and joy. The matter of the bath house. Nakedness was not an important thing in Russia. The coachman had not intended any disrespect. The Uncle, Pavel Borisovich, had probably not intended any disrespect. The matter of the torn photograph.

'What about the Fraülein, the German governess?' Mrs Graham asked. 'How did this Uncle Pavel get on with her?'

Miss Kinsman paused. 'They got on together very well.'

It was nearly time for Vespers. No church bells were allowed to ring in Moscow except from the Orthodox church itself. Mrs Graham was aware of the exact time, apparently without looking, as she sat with her back to the carriage clock. At three minutes to six she began to stir, and Frank said, 'I'd better be off now, Mrs Graham. There was something I'd wanted to talk to you about, but it can very well wait till another time.'

'I shouldn't have thought it could,' said Mrs Graham. She said goodbye to him in her distinctive manner, looking down for a moment at his hand in hers as though wondering where she'd got it from, then pressing it and looking into his eyes with an assurance that he would not be forgotten.

In the hallway a door opened and the Anglican chaplain, the Reverend Edwin Graham, came out.

'Ah, Reid. You're here, Reid. Nice to see you.'

A servant brought him his galoshes and his hat and cloak. The chaplain put them on, went back into his study, came out with a few sheets of typed paper fastened with a paper-clip, waved away the servant, who appeared again, thinking something more was wanted, looked round at Frank to see if he was coming to the service, waved the sheets of paper at him in ironic invitation, and made off across the square to the chapel. Frank too went off into the darkness.

He meant to go up to the Novinsky Boulevard and take a tram. That was the quickest way home, quicker, at this time in the evening, than a sledge. A senseless fear had come over him that if he stayed away too long, the children, once again, would be gone by the time he got back. Turning right up the Nikitskaya he looked round, for no very definite reason, and saw that Miss Kinsman was behind him, threading her way efficiently between the many pedestrians. There were no drunks on this respectable street, and she made rapid progress. In Frank's opinion, she ought to have gone to Vespers. But it struck him now that Mrs Graham, who could act very quickly if she thought fit, had told Miss Kinsman, during those few minutes while he was in the hall, about his difficulties. She had tipped Miss Kinsman the wink. Everyone knew that Nellie had gone, and on this delicate subject all, apparently, were experts. With the ruthlessness of the timid, Miss Kinsman was coming after him now to suggest that she would be suitable for the post of governess at 22 Lipka Street.

And perhaps she was right, but Frank didn't feel able to think about the whole thing, much less make up his mind, at the moment. He remembered that he had given something, twenty-five roubles in fact, to the collection for her expenses and her fare to Charing Cross. He didn't grudge that at all, but, all things considered, shouldn't it have let him off? He was known in Moscow, in both the Russian business community and the English one, as a just man. He hadn't anything, quite the contrary, against Miss Kinsman. But if she had it in mind, or had had it put into her mind, to move into his house and take charge of the family, there was Dolly to be thought of. Dolly's word was not 'just' but 'fair'. She would not think it fair of him to make any arrangement with Miss Kinsman. Miss Kinsman was dowdy, another of the words that couldn't be translated into Russian, because there was no way of suggesting a dismal unfashionableness which was not intentional, not slovenly, not disreputable, but simply Miss Kinsman's way of looking like herself. Frank had never pretended to be able to answer Dolly's objections, but he knew, for the most part, what they would be. On the other hand, what was there to stop him from letting Miss Kinsman overtake him and finding out from her quite clearly — for he could, after all, be wrong — exactly what she wanted?

There was nothing to stop him, but he turned into a side-street. He might as well go to the Povarskaya and catch his tram lower down the Boulevard. In that way he'd avoid Miss Kinsman, and would never have to speak to her at all. She wouldn't have to brood on the matter of Mr Reid's odd behaviour. Really it would be sparing her distress.

Everyone took short cuts in Moscow. The tram numbers, except for the line round the boulevards, were frequently changed, and unless you felt like paying for a sledge or a cab you were bound to spend a good deal of time on foot. But once you were off the main streets you had to know (since it could scarcely be explained) the way. Street names soon ran out. You were faced by towering heaps of bricks and drain-pipes, or a lean-to which encroached on the pavement, or a steaming cow-shed whose rotten planks seemed to breathe in and out under their own volition. All these things, which had no legal right to be there and were unknown to any map, had to be imagined away if you wanted to steer a true course. There might be no alternative to walking through one door of a temporary building and out at the other.

The turning Frank had reached was, he knew, Katsap Pereulok, although there was no trace of a sign. The passageway was filled, like a gully, with pearly darkness. There was a light on the corner, though not a municipal one, only a kerosene lamp fixed low on the wall. He looked back, Miss Kinsman, in her felt hat and winter overcoat, was just turning into the passage.

Not only good sense, but ordinary politeness told Frank that he must speak to this woman and offer to take her back to Povarskaya. She looked lamentably out of place in this unsavoury lane, struggling to put up her umbrella, although no snow was falling. But if she'd come as far as this, she must know the way back, and if she couldn't catch up with him, she could go back to the Chaplaincy. I shouldn't like to try and give a connected account of what I'm doing, he thought. I shouldn't, for example, like to give an account of it to Tvyordov. But I'm being hunted. She's hunting me down, like a bill-collector. Instead of turning right, back to the boulevards, he went left, through a narrow opening, towards the Kremlin. He was going twice as far as he needed to, because of this hunting process. But poor woman, surely she can't come much farther.

Kolbasov Pereulok. The name was painted up, but ahead of him access was narrowed down by towering piles of sacks on either side, as if the two houses opposite each other, dimly lighted, were in competition to block out each other's windows. There was a reek of tar and frying buckwheat pancakes (Frank sighed with hunger). Once into the lane, the ground floors of the houses became shops, with windows half below the pavement level. There was no way of telling what they dealt in. Very likely they were repair shops, there was nothing you couldn't get repaired in Moscow, a city which in its sluggish, maternal way cared, as well as for the rich, for the poorest of the poor. Bring me your broken shoes, your worn-out mattresses, your legless chairs, your head-less beds, and in some basement workshop or hole in the wall, I will make them serviceable, at least for a few months or so. They will be fit to use, or at least fit to take to the pawnbroker's.

On the corner there was a Monopoly, a government vodka shop. It was small, but brightly lit. Inside, a woman of great size and strength, wrapped in a black knitted shawl, sat on a stool behind a wooden partition with a small window in it, wired in, like a ticket office. There was nowhere to sit down. Men and women waited with empty bottles or leaned uncertainly against the wooden walls. The exact money had to be counted out before the taps behind the partition were unlocked.

Miss Kinsman, Frank was convinced, and the convic-tion came with a rush of relief, would never risk walking past this place. If she did she was an impostor, with no right to her felt hat and her dowdiness and the touching stories she had told at the chaplaincy. And it came to him that, more than anyone else he'd ever encountered in Moscow, Miss Kinsman was like his second cousin Amy in Nottingham, younger, but like cousin Amy, who crossed the road rather than go past a public house because she believed that if she did, the doors might open and men would stumble out to piss and inside she would glimpse women stabbing each other with hat-pins. Whether this really ever happened to his cousin he didn't know. He usually wrote to her regularly, as he did to all of them, but hadn't this month, and the slight physical sensation, not of guilt, but of feeling he ought to feel guilty, turned into a considerable irritation. Still he was almost in the clear now. The Monopoly, as usual, was on the corner of the main street, in case people started drinking on the premises, and the police had to be called in. He had come out on Znamenkaya, which when you considered that he ought to be home by now, was ridiculous. But he was free now and his mind went back to his own troubles, or rather let them rise from where they had been waiting to the surface.

He was heading towards the river, and the air was full of the vast reverberations of the bells from the five golden domes of the church of the Redeemer, not at anything like their full power, but like the first barrage of artillery before the main attack. The attack did not come – it was Lent, and they chimed only once, but they were answered from across the river by a hundred others, always with one chime only. He stood listening to the bells in the open starlight. From the cathedral square a ramp went down to the water. The river ran darkly, still choked with the winter's majestic breaking ice and the debris carried along with it, an inconceivable amount of rubbish – baskets, crates, way-posts, wash-tubs, wheels, cradles, the last traces of the traffic the ice had carried while, for four months, it was a high-road. Watching the breaking ice from the bridges was one of Moscow's favourite occupations. The *Gazeta-Kopeika* said that a pair of dead lovers, clutched together, had floated by, frozen into the ice. The *Gazeta* repeated this story every spring.

There was no bridge here, but from the towpath someone, at some time, had fenced off a piece of the river with wooden stakes. A dilapidated gangway led out from the towpath to a raft, floating on empty kerosene drums. It had a roof of sorts, and people fished there. Frank had often fished from it himself, without a permit, when he was a schoolboy. Up till March, of course, you had to make your own hole in the ice. Although he was in a hurry, the relief from tension made him slow down, and he walked down to the platform to watch the ice for a while. You had to get through the piled snow at the river's edge and then there was just a two-foot drop on to the sodden platform which oozed and creaked beneath you. He stood there, with the half-frozen wooden slats vibrating beneath him, and the church bells sounding more clearly, a kind of distant hum, as the Redeemer fell silent. Then he walked the length of the gangway. When he stopped he heard another, lighter creaking as Miss Kinsman jumped down behind him.

She came purposefully towards him, not out of breath, her umbrella folded now. Frank reflected that he was caught. The place was a kind of fish-trap anyway, he'd known that since he was ten, and now he was trapped himself and must put the best face on it he could.

'Have you been trying to catch up with me, Miss Kinsman? I'm afraid I didn't see you.'

The frosty night air was as keen as a needle. She stood there, and answered him mildly, without a hint of complaint.

'Yes, I have. I think you did see me.'

They were standing together under the ramshackle roof, and she was settling down like a fowl in a fowl-house, brushing off first one shoulder of her overcoat, then the other, although snow had not been falling.

'I'm afraid it must have meant coming through some rather rough-looking streets,' he said.

'Poor, but I shouldn't call them rough.'

'There was the Monopoly.'

'Oh, I don't mind the Monopolies. They're not like English public-houses. They're not allowed to drink on the premises, you know. They have to take the vodka at least a hundred metres away before they start drinking. And it's such stuff, have you ever tried it?'

Frank had. 'It does what it's always said to do, and what it's manufactured to do. That's the trouble, perhaps.'

'And the woman in there, she was a Tatar woman, that means she's a Muslim, you know, she's forbidden to drink by the Prophet. The Prophet, you know,' she repeated, nodding emphatically.

'But did you want to speak to me?' he asked, and added, 'about anything in particular?'

She looked at him closely and said 'No.'

'You've nothing to say to me?'

'Oh, you needn't have been afraid of that,' she added. 'I didn't want to talk to you, I wanted to talk to Mr Frank Reid.'

'Who did Mrs Graham say I was?' Frank asked.

'I didn't quite catch. So often one doesn't quite catch! And then she had to go to Vespers. But, you see, it's a matter of some urgency. Really, my passage for England is booked for tomorrow, if I can't find any other employment here, that is. All I need is his address, Mr Reid's address. That, of course, you must have, as you're one of the business community here, even though he must be a younger man than yourself.' She looked at him from the deeper shadow of her hat. 'I wouldn't have troubled you, only I should have to speak to him tonight.'

'What makes you think he's younger than I am?' Frank asked.

'He has young children, I know that. Otherwise I shouldn't need to speak to him.'

Frank considered for a moment.

'I'm sorry to disappoint you, Miss Kinsman, but I'm sure that this wouldn't be a good moment to speak to Frank Reid.'

'Is he out of Moscow, then?'

'Well—'

'Ultimately, you see, nobody is interested in me but myself. Certainly you, a total stranger, can't possibly be. But I have to make do with the material I have.'

'Miss Kinsman. I'm quite sure that if you did see Frank Reid, it wouldn't lead to anything. I know him quite well enough for that.'

She looked at him searchingly. He offered to see her back to the nearest tram-stop. She shook her head, and trudged off across the gangway and up the slippery ramp, towards the Redeemer. Until she was out of sight all he could do was to stand there like an idiot, pretending to watch the ice.

# 10

The next morning, as Frank discovered from ringing up the Chaplaincy, Miss Kinsman left very early for the Alexander station. Mrs Graham said 'Really, I expected to read something about you in the *Gazeta-Kopeika*. Everyone thought you were going to push her into the river.'

'Who's everyone? There was no-one there.'

'Oh, people on the towpath, you know.'

'What were they doing?'

'Watching the ice.'

'Mrs Graham, I got the impression that Miss Kinsman wanted to have a post with me in Lipka Street, as governess to my children.'

'Oh, I should never have suggested that myself. After all, I know why she had to leave her other place. The matter of the bath house.'

At lunchtime, at Reidka's, he tried to put his case – largely to put it to himself – to Selwyn, who said 'I don't remember a fishing-place like that near the Redeemer. I thought the banks were supposed to be kept clear.'

'It's surprising what the police will overlook if there's

no trouble. It's been there for twenty-five years at least, I expect they've got used to it. But it doesn't matter about the place. I can show it to you anytime you like. It's just that I feel I haven't behaved even reasonably well to this woman, but I don't know where she's going when she arrives in England, and if I did I shouldn't know what to do about it.'

'You're thinking of sending her money.'

'Money isn't such a bad thing as people make out.'

'It doesn't heal the spirit, Frank.'

Frank shifted his ground.

'I suppose she must be getting on for fifty. It doesn't seem a good time for disappointment. I suppose, I mean, if you're younger, there's more chance of things getting better.'

'How old are you, Frank?'

'That's another thing, she seemed to think I looked older than I am. Perhaps I do, I don't know.'

It was five o'clock. Selwyn locked the safe and the cupboard where the account books were kept and, although he was always due at some meeting or concert or other, sat down again to give counsel.

'Your difficulty in making up your mind what to do about Miss Kinsman is a reflection of your difficulty in deciding what to do about Nellie. Am I right in thinking that you don't know all her motives? And will you let me say that you would reach a conclusion more quickly if you considered yourself less — if you thought, as each solution presented itself — who will be wounded by this? and whose heart will be made lighter?'

'I'm thinking about my children,' said Frank. 'I was thinking about them when Nellie left. I thought about them when this woman tracked me down through the back streets of the Tverskaya. Who else is going to think about them?'

'Frank, give me your hand.'

Selwyn's hand was lean and spindle-fingered, the palm hardened by grasping his pilgrim's staff through hundreds of versts of summer tramping. He sighed, and gently let go again.

'Frank, not so very long ago I acted in a manner which I had never, up till then, considered excusable. I have known a number of people who acted in the same way, and though I would not have thought it right to condemn them, I would never have approved of what they did, and I would have done all I could to act in a like manner. The strange thing is that, as you know, I've been for a number of years now under the influence of Lev Nicolaevich, and have made up my mind, and indeed my whole being, towards a worthier mode of life and one which would be of more use to my fellow creatures. Yet now I was apparently reverting to a former attitude, one that I held when I was a younger man. I'm speaking of the sexual impulse, Frank, and its gratification.'

'Well, I thought you must be,' said Frank.

'At that time I thought that both men and women benefited from a multiplication of joyous relationships. But I had come to see how wrong that is. My predicament was, then, how to act in order to cause as little pain as possible and, above all, what I should tell the human beings concerned.'

'I don't know what you had to tell them,' said Frank.

'You would have been as puzzled as I was?'

'I'm puzzled as it is.'

'But I haven't distressed you by what I've been saying? You haven't taken offence?'

'How could anyone take offence at you, Selwyn? You might as well take offence at a drink of cold water.'

Selwyn gave a melancholy smile. 'We must go back to the subject later.' He seemed reluctant to leave, a symptom which Frank recognized at once. At length he said, in a lowered voice, almost reverent voice, 'How is it going, Frank? Has it been set up?'

He meant, Frank knew, the *Birch Tree Thoughts*. 'I'm trying to get the loan of some European type, Selwyn, you know that. Sytin's have some, but they won't lend it. We may have to try in Petersburg. Tvyordov will set it up for you, he won't mind what language it's in, and of course the boy won't be able to read the proofs, but I can leave that to you. We can hand-print it on the Albion.'

'The punctuation may give trouble, I know that. It happens that I —' he took a manuscript notebook out of his breast pocket, opened it — but it seemed to open itself at the required place — and handed it to Frank, who, aware that he hadn't been grateful enough for Selwyn's ready sympathy over Miss Kinsman, took it and read aloud:

> 'Dost feel the cold, sister birch?'
>     'No, Brother Snow,
> I feel it not.' 'What? not?' 'No, not!'

'Are you sure that's right, Selwyn?'

'What would you say is amiss?'

'I'm not quite sure.'

'Wasn't I successful in conveying my meaning?'

'It seems a bit repetitive.'

Selwyn took back the notebook, as though he did not like to see it in less expert hands, and Frank, saying that he'd lock up, was left alone in the darkened building, to look through the various offers of his paper suppliers. Paper from Finland was the cheapest by far, but the Tsar might decide to legislate against it. There was another offer, too, for the Mammoth, this time from Kuriatin, who thought he had discovered a purchaser in Tokyo, but as he had no licence to export, everything would have to be done through a third party.

This brought Frank's mind, for a moment, back to the

ruined crockery and tablecloths. He had discovered why Kuriatin set so much store by them. Like more important merchants than himself — Tretyakov, Kutzenov, Botkin — he had put aside part of his possessions to give to the People if necessary, thus showing his goodwill towards them.

'All for them, and the embroideries, and the pictures, and the portrait of my wife by Bogdanov-Belsky. Let the people treasure them, and let them remember Kuriatin!'

But there were other things he had earmarked to take with him if history turned against him and the family had to go into exile — the damask tablecloths, in particular, although there were only twenty-three of them. Before he came from his village in Orel, Kuriatin had never seen such things, not even on the altar at Easter.

# 11

'Certainly some woman must come into your house to care for your children,' said Selwyn, calling round that evening. 'When a woman leads a little child by the hand she ensures your future, just as when she serves you food and drink she bids you live.'

'She hasn't got to do that,' Frank said, 'but I want them kept happy, and they won't be happy running riot. And I want someone who'll speak good Russian to them. Their life is here in Moscow, for the time being anyway.'

'The young woman I have in mind speaks very pure Russian, Frank, in spite of everything.'

'In spite of what?'

'She has had some education, at one time they wanted to make a teacher of her. I'm sure she's capable of a responsible position. But she is unfortunate.'

'I don't want anyone too unfortunate about the place. What went wrong?'

'She is young—'

'How young?'

'I would say she is nineteen or twenty, and she is poor. There can be no higher claim on any of us, surely, than youth and poverty.'

'Where does she come from?'

'Vladimir.'

'Where they're mostly carpenters.'

'Yes, Lisa Ivanova is a joiner's daughter.' Selwyn moved his head very slightly from side to side, as though in time to music.

'Did you meet her in Vladimir?'

'No, I met her in Muir and Merrilees, at the handker-chief counter. Yes, she is in charge of the gentlemen's handkerchiefs. I told you that she could manage a respon-sible position.'

'You picked her up at Muirka's.'

'She was shedding tears. That was enough for me, as it should be for us all, for us all.'

'You mean she'd been fired?'

'Not at all, it was simply that she's not used to living in a great city, and she feels oppressed, like any other child of nature.'

'Did she tell you that?'

'No, that is what I sensed.'

'They pay them quite fairly at Muirka's,' said Frank. 'That's to say, as wages go here. And they get a discount on staff purchases. But I think I ought to try and find someone older and perhaps a bit more fortunate. She sounds as though she'd need looking after herself.'

'But you mustn't think of it as a question of your own convenience.'

'What else is it?'

'Try to put aside this consideration of self.'

Soothe him, Frank thought. 'Well, it wouldn't be for very long, in any case.'

'You've heard from Nellie, then?'

'I haven't heard.'

'You're expecting her back, though?'

'I'm always expecting her.'

'What am I to say, then, to Lisa Ivanova?'

'The worst thing about you, Selwyn, is that you make everyone else feel guilty. I feel guilty now. You'd better bring this girl to see me.'

'And when shall I do that?'

'Well, when does Muirka's shut? Half-past six. Bring her to the house, when she gets off work. I don't want her in the office. We'll have to see what she thinks of the children.'

'You have a good heart, Frank. Many men, most men I fancy, would have said, "We'll have to see what the children think of her," or even "We'll have to see what I think of her."'

'I don't want to have to think about her at all,' said Frank. 'I'm at the end of my wits.'

He had the impression that they were avoiding an

important aspect of the subject, but felt too tired to work out what it was.

When Selwyn brought Lisa into the living room at 22 Lipka Street, Frank thought that she looked less unpromising than he'd expected. How unjust, (or unfair) that was, to ask someone to live up to a promise about which they knew nothing, and yet that was what interviewing usually came down to. It was her hair that surprised him. As a shop assistant, she must have worn it rolled up. Old Merrilees would never permit anything else behind the counters. But her hair now, her thick fair hair, which gleamed in the electric light, pale blonde on one side, palely shadowed on the other, was parted in the middle and fell in two flaxen pigtails like a peasant's or rather like a peasant in a ballet. He didn't think he'd be able to put up with this.

She had the pale, broad, patient, dreaming Russian face, and it struck him that it reminded him of another face which he had seen recently, though he couldn't remember when or where. She wore her black shop assistant's dress with a lilac-coloured shawl over it, and plain gold rings in her ears. Selwyn's description of her had suggested that she might turn up fainting, possibly in rags, but when she took off her shawl she looked like any other employee at Muirka's.

Selwyn proposed that they should all sit down. Lisa

THE BEGINNING OF SPRING

Ivanova looked astonished, then her expression became serene and, once again, calmly receptive. She sat in the armchair nearest to her, which had always been Nellie's. But Lisa was taller, as well as broader, than Nellie, so that her head came almost to the top of the chair-back. She sat, not at all stiffly, but absolutely still, all, so to speak, in one piece. Nellie had never been much of a sitter-still. She was a jumper-up and walker-about.

When Frank spoke to Lisa directly she turned politely towards him, but her self-possession produced a curious effect, as though, in spite of the politeness, she was listening to something else a little beyond his range.

'Are you used to looking after children?' he began, but Selwyn, leaning forward, interrupted rapidly in English. 'Frank, I work as your accountant, as I did for your father before you, and I do my best in that capacity, but in the present matter you must think of me as an older brother.'

Lisa was not embarrassed by these remarks which she could not understand. Evidently she had the gift of quiet. She waited without any particular expression, but not with the passive air of someone about to be disposed of.

'All I ask,' Selwyn went on, 'is that you should make it clear that the atmosphere is one of hope, and that you have no shadow of doubt that you will soon be reunited with your own wife. I'm speaking to you freely.'

'I should have thought we could have taken that for granted.'

Selwyn subsided. Now that he saw everything was going well, his mind was turning to his next charitable enterprise. With the terrible aimlessness of the benevolent, he was casting round for a new misfortune.

Frank tried again. 'Lisa Ivan'na, are you used to looking after children? Have you ever done it before?'

'Yes, I have younger brothers and sisters.'

'Did you find it hard work?'

'It's hard work looking after one child. It's quite easy if there are several.'

'Is that so?' asked Selwyn, his attention caught. 'I should have thought the opposite.'

'Well, I've got three of them,' Frank persisted. 'You'll see them in a minute. My wife has been called away urgently to England. The youngest one needs looking after sensibly while the others are in school, and I suppose she might be taught a few letters and numbers. When they come back from school, at mid-day, they'll want to go skating, if the ice is holding anywhere, or a walk in the Prechistnaya.'

'Should you want me to live in this house?'

'Where are you living at the moment?'

'I'm in the female assistants' dormitory, on the top floor of Muir and Merrilees.' She added, 'I should prefer to live in your house.'

'We shan't need to go for a walk in the Prechistnaya,' said Ben, coming into the room. 'Dolly won't walk unless she's going somewhere, and there's only one place I want to go, and that's the Nobel garage in the Petrovka.'

'Go and fetch Dolly.'

'And Annushka?'

'Yes, and Annushka.'

Ben disappeared, and Selwyn got to his feet. 'Your decision is as good as made,' he said. 'I'll be on my way.' He was going to the Foundling Hospital. Wrong, of course, to feel impatient with him or to criticize him as he hurried, on errands of mercy, to the hidden rooms of the poor, the unlucky, and the bereaved into which he could pass, although a foreigner, with charmed steps. This, to be sure was partly because he was often thought to be touched by the finger of God.

As the three children came back, Annushka silent under Dolly's stern control, it struck Frank that they should be showing, so much more than they did, the effect of motherlessness. They ought either to be quieter or more noisy than before, and it was disconcerting that they seemed to be exactly the same. He would have been heartbroken if they had shown the least symptom of unhappiness, but was disturbed because they didn't. Annushka was, perhaps, wearing too many shawls and too many layers of clothing in the efficiently-heated house, and she had two holy medals round her neck now as well as her gold cross, but she looked pampered rather than neglected, and as if she were enjoying herself.

'This is Dolly,' he began.

'Dolly is Darya?' Lisa asked.

'Yes, Darya, Dasha, Dashenka. But I'm English, and I'm Dolly.'

'Dolly, this is Lisa Ivanovna. She's coming to look after you for, I don't know how long for, as long as is necessary, perhaps a few weeks, it might be longer than a few weeks.'

Dolly and Lisa, as was correct, shook hands, and the two self-contained creatures stood for a moment opposite each other, in the green-shaded lamplight, reserving judgement.

'Ben, shake hands with Lisa Ivanovna,' Frank said.

'Are you going to live in our house?' asked Ben.

'I think so.'

'It would be better if you made up your mind.'

'You don't know what would be better for me,' said Lisa equably. 'You've never seen me before.'

'Yes, I have. I've seen you at Muirka's.'

'At the handkerchief counter,' Dolly added.

'Have you ever noticed us?' Ben asked. 'We go there quite often.'

'No, I haven't. I'm sorry if I'm disappointing you.'

'You're not disappointing us,' said Dolly. 'We want to know whether you're observant or not.'

Frank felt that Lisa would find looking after the children easier if she got used to the way their minds worked. Nellie had said to him often that she didn't know where they got it from and that although she didn't want them to grow like her own family, she hoped that at least they'd grow less unlike other people's children. And yet she had left them, she had sent them back on the train from Mozhaisk, like parcels.

He suggested that Lisa should go and give notice to Muir and Merrilees, and take up her duties in Lipka Street next Monday.

'Yes, I must work my week out.'

'Bring all your things on Monday. You'll have a room to yourself here.'

She looked, for the first time, appalled, and he realized that she had never, either in her village or in Moscow, slept in a room by herself before.

The children had gone off to the kitchens, where he knew they would be demanding bread dipped in tea and joining in a discussion of Lisa Ivanovna. Voices could be heard, louder and softer as the kitchen doors opened and shut to admit more people. Perhaps children were better off without a sense of pity. And then again perhaps Lisa didn't need pity, and he remembered that Selwyn had been about to tell him, but hadn't reached the point of telling him, why he had said she was unfortunate, and why she had been in tears behind the counter at Muirka's.

They had settled her wages at four roubles, sixty-seven kopeks a week, the same as she'd been getting at the store, but with no deduction, of course, for board and lodging. Although he did not feel particularly proud of the offer, he could see that she thought it more than fair.

'There's only one other thing, Lisa Ivanovna. Your hair.'

'Yes?'

'I'd rather it wasn't in plaits.' He wasn't compelled to give a reason, and he didn't give one. She nodded to show that she understood. 'Is there anything more you want to ask me?'

'Yes, do you have a dacha?'

'Yes, we do have one, at Beryoznyk. The children like it, of course, but I don't go there much myself. I'd really prefer to get rid of it, it's so damp, but I don't have to think about that yet, it's still winter.'

'It's nearly spring.'

He hoped she wasn't going to start contradicting him, also that she might smile occasionally. What he couldn't imagine was her shedding tears, in Muirka's or anywhere else. The outside world didn't seem to make enough impression on her for that.

# 12

Frank rang up Kuriatin to ask him whether there was any further news of the Japanese offer for the Mammoth. 'If you can't get an export certificate I'll have to look elsewhere. I have to clear the land, then let the site and the workshops together. There's been an opportunity cost of three thousand roubles a year on that site ever since my father died. I'd rather sell, of course.'

'And the trees, what about the trees?'

'They go with the site, of course, but they're not much, a few willows and alders.'

'More than a few, Frank Albertovich.'

Like all merchants, and all peasants, Kuriatin was obsessed with the chance to cut down trees. A dream of buying the site had begun to torment him. As to the Mammoth, Frank had not expected a direct reply quite yet. But neither had he expected Kuriatin to change the subject abruptly, and to say, with a laugh which seemed to blast the fragile telephone system, 'And so you are suited? No more English governesses, no more old women.'

'I've found a girl, yes. She's not a governess.'

'Let me tell you a story from the district of Orel, from my part of the country,' shouted Kuriatin. 'What does it show? Why, simply the necessity of ruling in one's own house. A peasant took a young woman to wife . . .'

Kuriatin frequently told these stories, though, to do him justice, Frank had never heard him tell the same one twice. This might simply be because they weren't, as he always claimed they were, from the District of Orel, but invented to suit the occasion.

'With a hundred other women to choose from he took a lazy one, a lazy girl who did everything in the house as badly as possible, and made him sell his horse to buy her fine clothes. Meanwhile the bread she made was so heavy that it had to be thrown to the pig, and the pig died in great pain. And the linen she spun was so coarse that when the husband got into bed with his wife the sheets tore off his skin. In the end he said to the woman, "You have caused me to sell the horse, the pig is dead and you have borne no children. So now you can get between the shafts and live on oats and rye, and do a horse's work." In this way he showed he was master in his own house. Remember that story, because there's a great deal of benefit to be got from it.'

'There's no benefit at all,' Frank replied. 'I object to it in principle and in detail.'

'You don't understand it. You have no peasants in England, and therefore no stories.'

'We have plenty of stories,' said Frank, 'but the woman always comes off best.'

'All the more reason to remember this one.'

At the Press the work went forward with a satisfactory lack of incident, making a pattern of its own, from the entries in the order book through to the finished orders, checked, counted and stacked for delivery. There was only one problem, he told Tvyordov, and that was the European type for the hand-printing of *Birch Tree Thoughts*. Still, there were several places he hadn't tried yet.

Tvyordov was distributing, and went on rattling back the type, without looking at the labels, while the difficulty was put to him. Apparently it did not interest him, or rather there was something else which interested him more. Still rattling away, he said, 'A man lives under the rule of nature. He can't look after children, and he can't live alone.'

'Why not?' Frank asked. 'Selwyn Osipych lives alone.'

'Perhaps, but he's a man of God.'

'I can't see why a man shouldn't live alone, whoever he is, as long as he stays sober.'

'That's what you say, Frank Albertovich, but your wife left only a few days ago and you've taken a woman into your house already.'

Tvyordov said this in no spirit of reproach. When you

looked at it, his opinion was not very different from Kuriatin's.

Far more important, as far as Frank's peace of mind was concerned, was the judgement of the household in Lipka Street. This depended on Toma and the cook, and to some extent on the yard dog, Blashl, a loyal but very foolish animal whose attachments were intense. The yardman had no opinion apart from Blashl's. Toma, speaking for all, but without explaining how they reached their conclusions, reported to Frank that they would be glad to welcome Lisa Ivanova next Monday.

'Well, did she come?' Frank asked that evening. The children were waiting round the supper table, which was already laid with several kinds of bread and a dish for cold boiled cabbage dressed, as it was Lent, with sunflower oil instead of butter. Ben was complaining that Annushka wanted, against all precedent, to say grace. 'Oh Lord Jesus, who with five loaves and two fishes,' gabbled the stoutly-built little girl.

'She doesn't understand what she's talking about,' said Ben.

Frank was overcome with the same uneasiness that he had felt when the Chaplain had waved his sermon at him, amiably enough, but without expectations. Luke-warm, but not quite cold, unbelieving, but not quite disbelieving, he had fallen into the habit of not asking himself what he thought.

'It won't do any harm if she says grace,' he said.

'It doesn't mean anything,' said Dolly, looking up for the first time. 'My teacher says there is no God.'

'I never heard anything about this before.'

'Oh, Lord Jesus, who with five loaves . . .' persisted Annushka.

'I have a different teacher this year,' said Dolly. 'Last year, we had Anastasia Sergeevna, this year we have Katya Alexeevna.'

'She's ugly,' said Ben, 'she's got enough black hair on her arms to stuff a mattress.'

Dolly ignored him. 'She's thought about everything for a long time, and she says there is no God.'

Lisa came into the room. She turned towards Frank, simply to make sure who was supposed to be keeping order, but the gesture seemed to be enough in itself, and the children, who had really wanted to fall silent, fell silent. So too did Frank, because Lisa had cut off her hair. Perhaps she had got someone else to cut it off for her, because it seemed to have fallen acceptably into shape.

'That's how my teacher's hair is cut,' said Dolly. Frank was not sure whether the resemblance frightened her, or not.

Quiet had descended, the room was at peace, and everybody sat down to eat. Frank tried to avoid looking at Lisa. Cutting her hair had made a great difference to her appearance. Her great beauty was her eyes, which were not particularly large and quite close together, but a long oval in shape and dark grey in colour, with dark lashes, the lower lid raised a little, as though she was always expecting to look into a bright light. It must be awkward for her at first, with all of them sitting round. When he did take a glance at her, though, it occurred to him how much a person's face changes at mealtimes. Lisa's face, so pale, so placid, so undisturbed even by speaking and smiling, was distorted now by the large piece of white bread she had crammed in, and her right cheek jutted out while her fine young jaws moved mechanically to and fro and her white throat dilated in the task of swallowing potato soup. 'Well, the girl's got to keep alive,' he thought. And it might be that she was hungry. Certainly Lisa wasn't worried by what he might be thinking of her. Perhaps she thought that he ought to be satisfied with her as she was, or more likely she wasn't thinking of him at all. After all, she had been hired, on a temporary basis and for an agreed weekly wage, to look after the children. And with her beautiful hair gone, she ought to look less interesting. He wished that this was so.

Toma brought in a platter of the fish from which the soup had been made, and set it on the sideboard. Like the soup tureen, it was one of the set Nellie had brought with her, first to Germany, then to Moscow — Staffordshire, given to them by Charlie. It had been held up at the customs for goodness knows how long, because the removal people had wrapped it in English newspapers, and they'd had to wait until the Russian censors had read, or said they had read, every line and every word.

Off came the lid of the tureen with a wild escape of steam, smelling of fish like a wharf at sunset. Each of them had a plateful except Annushka, who had a small saucer, not part of the set. She began to wail.

'You oughtn't to be here at all,' Dolly told her. 'We love you, but you're superfluous.'

Annushka cried more loudly, and Lisa got up silently and led her out of the room.

'Keep something hot for Lisa Ivanovna,' said Frank.

When they were out of the room he took the opportunity to ask Dolly about her new teacher.

'Doesn't the priest come round classes?'

'Oh, Batiushka!' said Dolly. 'Yes, he comes round, but he's afraid of women politicals. He's afraid of my teacher.'

'If she was a political she wouldn't be working at your school.' It seemed, however, that this teacher had spent some time the year before in exile, as a suspected person, in a village somewhere on the river Yemtsa. 'The government allowed her thirteen roubles a month, and a grant for extra winter clothes, but she didn't buy any.'

'She's dowdy,' said Ben.

'You only get eight roubles as an exile if you're of

peasant origin,' Dolly went on. 'But then, of course, you can earn money working in the potato fields.'

'Lisa Ivanovna's of peasant origin,' said Ben. 'That's her status. It's on her papers.'

'Have you been looking at them?'

'No, we asked her.'

'That's enough,' said Frank.

'It'll be all right when she comes downstairs again,' said Dolly. And indeed a curious peace entered the room with Lisa, curious to Frank because he felt it, at the same time, a disturbance. She had put Annushka to bed, and as she began to eat her fish, Frank saw that he was right, and she had been hungry. 'But there's no need for that,' he thought. The assistants had to pay for their meals at Muirka's, but the staff restaurant was subsidized, like his own canteen at the Press. If she hadn't had enough to eat there, whose fault was it but hers, and what had she spent her wages on? To keep the conversation going, he said, 'I see you've had your hair cut, Lisa Ivanovna.'

'We all of us wish you hadn't,' said Ben.

'Well, if I made a mistake, it will grow again,' said Lisa.

She ought to look at him, it seemed to Frank, with some kind of bewilderment or reproach, or at least put her hand up to the back of her head which was what all women did when their hair was mentioned.

'You look like a student,' said Ben. 'All you need is my gun.' He produced a toy revolver, made of wood and tin. 'It's a Webley, that's what all the students have now. I got it at the Japanese shop near the Kuznetsky Bridge.'

'I thought they sold kites there,' said Frank.

'They do,' said Ben. 'I don't want a kite.'

'Lisa cut off her hair because you didn't like it the way it was when she first came here,' said Dolly. 'You ought to say something about it.'

'I imagine Lisa doesn't want to sit here and listen to these remarks,' said Frank. 'Who would? I certainly shouldn't.'

'I don't mind being told that I look like a student,' said Lisa. 'I should like to have studied. But I shouldn't want to look like something that I'm not.'

– How could you look like something that you aren't? – Frank wanted, not to cry out, but to observe quite calmly. – What you are, Lisa Ivanovna, is solid flesh inside your clothes, within arm's length, or nearly, in all the glory of solid flesh, lessened a bit by your idiotically cutting off your hair – you must have known that wasn't what I meant, so why did you let them take the scissors to you? – lessened a bit perhaps, but solid still. But I can only recognize what's solid by touching it, which in this particular case, to be honest, would be by no means enough.

'What did you do with it?' asked Ben. 'Did you sell it? You have to have it off if you've had typhoid, but then it isn't worth anything.'

Before he shut up the house for the night Frank took the opportunity to say to Lisa, 'I'm sorry you never managed to study, if that's what you wanted to do. If you need help, or if you need anything else, anything at all, please ask me.' He expected her to reply with the well-tried phrases 'You're very good,' or 'you're a good man, Frank Albertovich,' but instead she said that there were people who needed help more than she did. That's unquestionably true, he thought, and perhaps I'm one of them. But he felt disconcerted.

# 13

There was nothing wrong, nothing that you could lay a finger on, in the way Selwyn did his work at Reidka's, but the imminent birth of his first volume had unsettled him. Middle-aged poets, middle-aged parents, have no defences. When the *Birch Tree Thoughts* were printed, sewn, bound, pressed and distributed to the better-class book-shops on the Lubyanka, he would have anxieties, but at least they would be different ones. Meanwhile, however, he had begun to speak of a German version — which would mean borrowing yet another set of type — and a Russian one. It was these two projects which had driven Frank to the idea of taking on a second accountant. The profits at Reidka's would just about bear the additional salary. He had had to do this without hurting Selwyn's feelings, but Selwyn was not a vain man.

'You understand that Bernov will be the costing accountant, something we've never had. He won't be concerned with the management, though we'll have to listen to his advice.'

'Yes ... yes ... where did you find him, Frank?'

'He's coming to us from Sytin's, a very small firm after a very big one, but I daresay that'll give him more opportunity.'

'From Sytin's! He'll find it another world. When is he coming to the Press?'

'I've got him down for the 27th of March, Russian calendar.'

'Excellent, excellent . . . But, Frank, that's the Feast of St Modestus. There'll be the blessing of the office ikon.'

'Not till the afternoon, they've agreed to work normal hours till four. It's not a church holiday. We'll have all day to show Bernov how we do things.'

Frank knew that Selwyn ought to have been present when he interviewed the alert, ambitious, bright-eyed Bernov, and he felt a pang of shame when Selwyn put only one more question: 'Would you say that this young man has been touched to any extent by the teachings of Tolstoy?' He had to say that he didn't know, but thought it unlikely.

'But you wouldn't call him a quarrelsome fellow?'

'He didn't quarrel with me when I saw him.'

All that had been fixed before Nellie went away, in what, if time were space, would be a different continent. Every day he sent her a letter which, for 8 kopeks, included a blank reply form. He had mentioned that there was a girl now, a Russian girl, to look after the children. He had, of course, no address for Nellie except

Charlie's, where he imagined the envelopes piling up in the hall under the multi-coloured light from the stained glass window above the front door. Dolly and Ben also wrote once, and Annushka added a wavering Russian A. Frank did not know what Dolly had put, and thought it dishonourable to try to find out. She had asked him how 'irresponsible' was spelled. But this letter, too, would come to rest in the hall, in Charlie's brass dish.

'You lose your wife, you take on a new clerk,' Kuriatin shouted down the telephone, to which he'd never got accustomed. 'Why do you need more staff?'

'You'd be just as suspicious if I got rid of the lot of them,' said Frank.

'It's only that I understand the printing business. The great ones are expanding, the little foreigners like you have to watch out for themselves.'

'You don't understand printing in the least, Arkady Filippovich. You'd have been exactly the same if it had never been invented.'

'I want to see you. We will speak of all these things at Rusalochka's.'

'We can speak, if you like,' said Frank. 'But at Rusalochka's we shan't be able to hear each other.'

During the forty-nine days of Lent entertainments were supposed to be cut down, and some of Moscow's restaurants were closed, but not Rusalochka's, the tea-rooms attached to the Merchants' Club. 'Come to Rusalochka's,' repeated Kuriatin, 'we will settle our business there once and for all.'

Frank tried as far as possible to avoid this place, which conflicted with his idea of what was sensible and his preference for a quiet life. Since it was supposed to be devoted to tea-drinking, the walls were frescoed from smoky ceiling to floor in red-gold and silver-gold and painted with dancing, embracing and tea-swilling figures overlapping with horses, horse-collars with golden bells, warriors, huts prancing along on chickens' legs, simpering children, crowned frogs, dying swans, exultant storks and naked women laughing in apparent satisfaction and veiled, to a slight extent, by the clouds of a glowing sunset. Service at Rusalochka's was in principle a simple matter, since nothing was served but tea, cakes, vodka and *listofka, slievanka, vieshnyovka* and *beryozovitsa*, the liqueurs of the currant-leaf, plum, cherry and birch-sap. But the great silver tea-pots, each like a kettle-drum on its wheeled stand, crossed and recrossed the aisles between the tables, which became smaller and smaller as the room filled up, only avoiding collision with each other and the trollies of strong alcohol through the manipulation of the waiters, who seemed to be chosen for strength rather than skill, and as a result of the threats and warnings of the customers bellowing either for further orders or, as it seemed, to encourage the racing tea-pots, as in a sporting event. The customers registered only as the opening and closing of mouths, all sound and sense being drowned by Rusalochka's mighty Garmoniphon, the great golden organ which with its soaring array of Garmonica pipes occupied the whole of one wall of the demonic tea-rooms. A German in a frock-coat played it, or perhaps a series of Germans in frock-coats, closely resembling each other. At home, the merchants preferred the old Russian songs, but not here, not at Rusalochka's, a very expensive place, by the way, where one saw and was seen, and where first Grieg and then Offenbach's *Belle Hélène* were now being played at the pitch of a dockyard in full production. And yet Kuriatin, if he wished to, was able to make himself heard.

'I've come here because you asked me to,' said Frank, drawing up a massive gilded chair. 'But I hadn't forgotten what it was like.'

He was well aware that Kuriatin had invited him to Rusalochka's partly as a joke, a joke which would be allowed to develop according to its natural direction. At the same time, he had genuinely intended a treat, believing that Frank, in his ordinary business day, never encountered anything as overwhelming as the Garmoniphon. But Kuriatin could not rest easy with this, because business intruded, and even if he made or negotiated an offer for the Mammoth he would feel he had missed something if he had no option on the Reid site, and its buildings, and its trees. Above all he had the suspicion that Frank was not, after all, impressed by Rusalochka's (although many of the decorations had been carried out in real gold leaf), and pity for Frank on account of this and, warring with the pity, envy.

What, in heaven's name, was Selwyn doing at Rusalochka's? The premises were barred against anyone but merchants and their guests, and yet there he was, making his way, wavering but unchallenged, towards their table. 'I wanted to have a few words with Frank Albertovich. I asked at his house and they told me that he had an engagement here.'

'Sit down, sit down, Selwyn Osipych,' Kuriatin cried, 'sit down, my dear friend,' then as Selwyn smiled and looked round him vaguely, but did not sit down, 'You don't want to sit with me!' Selwyn, whose appearance was just as bizarre as ever, could be of no possible importance to him, financially or socially, and yet Kuriatin trembled from head to foot with eagerness. 'You don't want to sit with me, it distresses you to see a man spend money at Rusalochka's. You'll tell me that in the villages the peasants have been taking the thatch off their roofs this winter to feed their cattle, and no doubt that's true. But in Russia who is happy?'

'No, no, you're wrong,' said Selwyn mildly, 'I don't criticize what you're doing. How can I criticize a life I don't understand? And surely you are happy.'

'It's true, it's true. When I die, God will say to me,

well, I gave you a life on earth, Arkady Filippovich, and what's more, a life in Russia. Did you enjoy it? And if not, why have you wasted your time?'

'What did you want to talk to me about, Selwyn?' asked Frank, as quietly as possible. 'Couldn't it wait? For God's sake sit down, in any case, if you're going to stay here.'

But Selwyn, looking round at the golden and copper walls, the threatening organ-loft, the perilous circulation of the waiters, the bloated, steaming and streaming customers to whom an attendant was now bringing hot towels, in the Chinese style, to wipe their drenched foreheads, gently shook his head. The effect on Kuriatin was immediate. Laying his hand on Selwyn's arm he began to plead, almost to wheedle.

'A nice glass of something . . . a samovar, a samovarchik, a dear little samovar . . . I can call for anything here, there is currant cake, Dundeekeks, as in Scotland . . .' Lumbering up from his seat he folded Selwyn in his arms and kissed him as high as he could reach, on the chin, while one of the mobile tea-pots, on a straight course past the table, swerved and missed him narrowly.

Disengaging himself, Selwyn nodded at Frank and made his way out of Rusalochka's. Kuriatin subsided.

'You sounded like a rich man in the Bible when the prophet comes in,' said Frank, 'I know you're doing quite well, but you're not rich enough to carry on like this.'

'Selwyn Osipych was like a reproach to me. He didn't intend it, of that I'm sure, but, yes, he has acted as a reproach. Now I feel I don't want to withhold anything from you.' At this point the organ redoubled its volume and even Kuriatin had to raise his voice. 'I shall withhold nothing!'

How could Selwyn, in a couple of inconclusive minutes, have raised, quite unintentionally, such trust and repentance? It was a gift that would have been of inestimable value to him in business, if Selwyn had ever done any.

'I invited you here,' said Kuriatin, still in tears, 'in the way of business, without good intentions. I was lying to you when I said I couldn't obtain permits to export the Mammoth. I saw that delay was likely to bring me increased profits.'

'Of course you were lying,' Frank replied. 'I came here mainly to tell you that I've managed to negotiate the permits from the Ministry of Internal Affairs and the Ministry of Transport myself. I'd have been happy for you to do the job, but I can't wait any longer, I've got to have the site clear, either for rent or sale.'

At the words 'rent or sale' Kuriatin looked for a moment like his usual self, but then his eyes filled with tears again and he declared that the details no longer mattered to him.

'Just because Selwyn Osipych came in, and wouldn't sit down at the table?'

'Ah, you don't know what I was like in childhood, Frank Albertovich. The thought of a man's childhood can touch his soul, even when it's hard as flint. I've got photographs of myself as a child, poor faded things, but they show me as I was then, sitting in a little goat-cart.'

'How long do you think your change of heart will last?' Frank asked, thinking of various other dealings outstanding between them.

'Who can tell?' Kuriatin pushed the bottles on the table away from him.

Frank went downstairs, retrieved his overcoat, and escaped from the overpowering heat and noise and the improbable sight of the merchant's repentance. As he reached the Redeemer, a down-and-out of some kind moved up to him out of the shadow of one of the porches in the southern wall. Near the great churches the police never moved the beggars away, nor did anyone want them to. Frank stopped to take out his reserve of twenty-five kopek pieces, which were always at the ready. It was Selwyn, however, in his tattered sheepskin.

'I have been waiting for you Frank. I couldn't speak to you in the presence of Kuriatin.'

'In that case I can't think why you turned up at Rusalochka's at all.'

'I hoped you might come away with me.'

'Well, I was there on business. Is there anything wrong?'

Their breaths rose together as steam into the bitterly cold lamplit air, Selwyn's fainter than Frank's.

'I went back to the Press, Frank, after it closed. I had the keys, as you know, this evening, as you had to leave early for your appointment. I went back because I hadn't had the oppportunity during the day to see how far they'd got with . . .'

'With your poems.' He could, of course, have asked Tvyordov, but Selwyn, Frank knew, was in awe of Tvyordov.

'Yes, yes, with *Birch Tree Thoughts*.' Selwyn pronounced his title, as always, in a different and sadder tone, which in England would be reserved for religious subjects.

'The Birch Tree Thoughts are all right,' said Frank. 'You can have the first printing when you go in tomorrow. I told them to leave seventy-five copies in the compositors' room, to keep them separate from the deliveries. You could have taken them away tonight if you'd gone in there. I can't see why you didn't.'

'Ah, that was what I came to tell you, Frank. There were lights on in the building.'

'Didn't you see that the lights turned off when you left?'

'Let me be more specific. There was one light on, Frank, one light in the building, I think the light of a candle, moving from one window to another.'

'Well, who was it?'

'That I fear I can't tell you. I didn't go in to see.'

'Do you mean you left them to it, whoever it was?'

'I didn't know who it was carrying the light, Frank. It might have been a man of violence. I am a man of peace, a man of poetry.'

Selwyn seemed to be murmuring something, perhaps a blessing. 'Every single man that's born into this life, Frank, writes poetry at some time or other. Possibly you may not have done so yet.'

'Listen, Selwyn. Are you taking in what I'm saying?'

'Yes, indeed.'

'In the first place, give me the keys.'

'The keys to the Press?'

'The keys to the Press.'

Selwyn hesitated, as though struck by doubt or inspiration, and then handed them over.

'Now, either go round to 22 Lipka Street, or telephone them, and tell them I'll be late back, later than I said I would. Is that clear, and are you sure you won't forget to tell them?'

'Yes, yes, I'll speak to Lisa Ivanovna.'

'Just tell her what I've said.'

It was the worst season of the year in Moscow to hurry anywhere. The sledges were off the streets, there was still too much ice for taxis, nothing for it but a cab. It was the eve of a Saint's Day, so that all fares would be doubled.

What Frank expected to find at the Press he didn't know. In the cab he tossed up, Tsar or Eagle, with one of his twenty-five kopek pieces. Eagle, and he'd stop at a police station and get hold of an inspector to come with him. Tsar, he'd go on by himself. He went on by himself.

# 14

At Reidka's, a glimmer of light still showed in the window of the compositors' room. Frank negotiated the rows of trolleys waiting for tomorrow's delivery boys and tried the main entrance door. It was unlocked. He went upstairs, not troubling to walk either quietly or noisily.

A young man, still wearing his overcoat, was sitting with his back to the room on one of the compositors' stools with a lighted candle in front of him. He might almost have been asleep, but he suddenly pulled himself up straight and turned towards Frank a pale reproachful student's face. His blond eye-lashes gave him a bemused look, as of something new-born, but he wasn't too dazed, as the electric light came on, to blow out the candle. Probably he had always had to economize.

'You have found me.'

'I wasn't looking for you, though,' said Frank. 'Who are you?'

The young man pulled out of his over-coat pocket an automatic about six inches long which might, like Ben's, be a toy, or might be a Webley. That's what students have these days. There was nowhere to hide a gun in a student's regulation high-buttoned jacket, they had to keep them in the right-hand coat pocket. He got to his feet and fired twice. The first shot went far wide of Frank into the opposite wall, where it dislodged a quantity of plaster. The second, wider still but at closer range, struck the upper wooden case of Tvyordov's frame, smashed it to bits, discharged the small capitals in a metal cascade on to the floor, then ricocheted off through the very centre of his white overall where it hung ready and buried itself behind the frame.

'You see! You see I didn't mean to hit you!'

'I don't know whether you meant to or not!' said Frank. He walked forward, put his forearm under the young man's chin and against his throat, and pushed. He had learned to do this as a boy in the yard of Moscow 8 School (Modern and Technical). Then he took the automatic out of his hand, shut the safety catch, and looked at it.

'You want to keep these properly cleaned,' he said. 'Otherwise the trigger spring breaks and it goes on firing until its empty.'

The student, doubled up, was coughing. Frank fetched him a glass of water from the tap at the sink in the corner.

'Is this water safe?'

'It's what my staff drink.'

'I feel better. My name is Volodya Vasilych. My last name I don't give.'

'I didn't ask for it.'

'These are your premises, Frank Albertovich. You want to know what I'm doing here.'

'I'm sure you'll tell me in time. I take it you're a student?'

'Yes.'

'A student of what?'

'Of political history.' Frank wondered why he'd bothered to ask. He said, 'Meanwhile I shall have to account for all this mess and destruction to my chief compositor when he comes in the morning.'

Without any awkwardness Volodya dropped on to all fours and began to pick up the type.

'No, leave it,' said Frank. 'It has to go in the right place or not at all. What I really want to know is how you got in here.'

'The door wasn't locked.'

'Didn't that surprise you?'

'Nothing surprises me.'

From downstairs a voice called out: 'Sir, shots have been heard coming from your premises.'

It was the night watchman. Nothing on earth would bring him upstairs if there was a chance of being fired at. Altogether he was a sensible fellow.

'Everything's all right, Gulianin.'

'Good, sir. Very good.'

Gulianin retreated. 'Doubtless he'll fetch the street police,' said Volodya.

'Doubtless he won't. He'll wait to see how much I give him in the morning.'

Volodya, who seemed to have prepared what he had to say, repeated, 'My name is Volodya Vasilych.'

'So you told me.'

'I only shot at you to demonstrate that I was serious. Let me explain. You are a printer, Frank Albertovich.'

'I don't deny that. Did you want something printed?'

'I'm used to working a hand-press, but I no longer have access to one. I thought that if I could find a hand-press here I could get what I needed, only a couple of pages, done in a few hours. But you have no shutters here and I can't work without light, which means I can't conceal myself.'

'I can see that's awkward for you. But you could have come and given us an order, you know, in the usual way. However, I must warn you, that we don't do anything political.'

'What I have written is not political.'

'What's the subject?'

'The subject is universal pity.'

Volodya's expression was strained, as though he had entered his remark for an important prize, and could hardly believe that he wouldn't receive it.

'Well, then, you could have asked us for a quotation,' said Frank, 'I mean, just for the two pages. It would have saved a good deal of time and damage, and I don't think you'd have found our price unreasonable.'

'Prices . . . I don't know anything about that,' Volodya murmured, and then, after a pause for reflexion, 'it's possible that what I wanted to print might be considered as political.'

'I suppose that would depend on who's being universally pitied,' said Frank. 'Have you got your copy with you?'

Volodya hesitated. 'No, I have committed it to memory.' Then he made a wide gesture with both arms, as if he was scattering food for hens, and cried: 'But after all, what can that matter to you? You're a foreigner, the worst that you could suffer, if things didn't go right, would be expulsion from Moscow back to your own country. A Russian can't live away from Russia, but to you it's nothing.'

Frank had long ago got used to being asked, usually by complete strangers, for assistance. They were convinced that, as a business resident in good standing, he could help with their external passports or with permissions of some kind, or else they wanted him to delay their military conscription or to threaten their college superintendent into giving them better marks, or to sign a petition to the Imperial Chancery about a relative who had fallen into disgrace. Sometimes they wanted to borrow small sums of money to tide them over, or larger ones to help them train as a doctor or an engineeer. He had a reputation for doing what he could, otherwise these people wouldn't have gone on coming to him, but all of them, at one point or another, reminded him that he was a foreigner who, even if things didn't go right, had nothing to lose.

'What makes you think it wouldn't matter to me if I had to leave Russia?' he said. 'I was born here, I've lived here most of my life, I love Moscow at all seasons, even now at the beginning of the thaw, and I'm a married man with three children.'

'Yes, but your wife has left you.'

Volodya spoke confidently, but seemed to realize that he was not making exactly the impression he had intended.

'Where do you live?' Frank asked him.

'A long way out. In the Rogozhskaia.'

'Go back there.'

'But my property . . .'

'Not the gun. Here's the candle, if you brought it with you. Don't come here again.'

As Frank took a last look round the room, he noticed the seventy-five copies of *Birch Tree Thoughts*, still neatly piled and undisturbed by Tvyordov's frame.

'Take this as a souvenir,' he said to Volodya, handing him the top copy.

Volodya put the book in his now empty pocket and loped away down the stairs. Frank switched off and locked up. Impossible to repair Tvyordov's upper case, or the bullet-hole in his apron. Impossible, too, to estimate the effect on Tvyordov, when he reported for work next day, of the defilement and disturbance. That was a problem for the morning, and there were likely to be others. Open the doors, the Russians say, here comes trouble.

On the way back he went down to the iron bridge, the Moskvoryetszkevya, where passers-by were still watching the ice, and threw the little gun into the river. Then he walked home with a reasonably clear conscience.

In the living room Dolly and Ben were still, apparently, finishing their homework. A twenty-five watt bulb, the strongest that could be bought in Moscow, hung over their table, Dolly's brown exercise book, Ben's pink one. Dolly was tracing a map, a mildly hypnotic process. Her nickel-plated nib scratched industriously. Outside the circle of light, Lisa was sewing. Frank would have thought that the light wasn't good enough there and that all this sewing might have been done by somebody else in the house. There was a little room fitted up with a Singer off the kitchen passage. Perhaps Lisa wanted to show that she wasn't quite a governess and not quite a servant. Perhaps she didn't want to show anything, and they were all passing a peaceable evening without him.

'You're late,' Dolly said.

'Didn't Selwyn Osipych telephone you?'

'Yes,' said Dolly reluctantly, 'but Lisa answered, and she didn't tell us how long you'd be.'

'He didn't tell me either, Dolly.'

'Well, we were waiting,' Dolly said. 'Ben got rather restless.'

'I'll tell you why I'm late, it's nothing to worry about. There was someone at the Press, someone hanging about who shouldn't have been there. I went to see what was going on. Don't worry, it wasn't a thief.'

Dolly seemed mildly disappointed.

'If it wasn't a thief, who was it?'

'He was a student, I think.'

'Don't you know?' Dolly asked. 'You never used to be like this.'

'He said he was a student.'

'What did he want?'

'I'm not quite sure.'

'What was he called?'

'Volodya something-or-other.'

'Where has he gone?'

'Back home, as far as I know.'

'Will he come back?' Lisa asked. Frank met her clear, blank gaze. He felt pleased to have aroused even this much interest.

'I think it's very unlikely. I'm afraid the whole outing must have been a great disappointment to him, and I don't think he'll have any further business at the Press.'

'I can't see why he had to come so late anyway,' said Ben. 'Were you angry with him?'

'Not at all, I gave him a present.'

'Do you think he's got a gun?'

'Not now.'

# 15

When Frank had been a small boy and they had lived on the site, the first sign of spring that couldn't be mistaken had been a protesting voice, the voice of the water, when the ice melted under the covered wooden footpath between the house and the factory. The ice there wasn't affected by the stoves in the house or the assembly-shop furnace, the water freed itself by its own effort, and once it had begun to run in a chattering stream, the whole balance of the year tilted over. At the sound of it his heart used to leap. His bicycle came out of the shed and he oiled it out of a can which was no longer frozen almost solid. In a few weeks the almond trees would be in flower and the city would be on wheels again.

The day after the break-in, he allowed himself, as he had done then, to expect the spring. He knew he had an awkward day ahead, although he'd always thought, until the last week or so, that he enjoyed difficulties. Perhaps he still did. What kind of day it would be for the new cost accountant seemed uncertain. Before that began he had to think of Tvyordov, for whose sake he was coming in early through the snow-patched streets.

Outside the Press he found two fourteen-year-old apprentices who had, until work began, nowhere else to go. They were arguing over a boat-shaped piece of wood in the gutter and as to which direction it would be swept in when the current unfroze.

'Listen,' said Frank. 'I'm sending both of you with a message to the chief compositor.'

He had decided what to do while he was having a shave at one of the many barbers who opened at five o'clock in the morning. 'Look at this letter. Read me the address on the envelope.'

The smaller boy read out, 'Chief Compositor I. N. Tvyordov, Kaluga Pereulok 54.'

'Do you know where that is?'

'Yes, sir.'

'Go together, keep an eye on each other, knock at the door, take a message if there is one from the chief compositor, and come back here within the half-hour.'

In the letter he had told Tvyordov that there had been a break-in at the Press during the night, so that the work would be interrupted, and there would be no need for him to check in until the next day, when everything would continue as usual. Pay for the missed day would be maintained. On the whole, Frank considered his message as untruthful — there had been no break-in, it was quite clear that Selwyn had forgotten to lock up — and cowardly, since it was only deferring an awkward moment. On the other hand, to confront Tvyordov, without any warning, with the ruin of his apron and his upper case would be inhuman, and at the same time Frank had to bear in mind that it was the feast of St Modestus, the patron saint of printing, and it was his duty to see that the blessing of Reidka's ikons went through, if possible, without disturbance. He had also to consider the night watchman, Gulianin, who had heard shots, but must be persuaded that he hadn't. With this in mind Frank had brought a reasonable sum of money in notes.

The night watchman, however, couldn't immediately be found. He lived over Markel's Bar, a few doors down from the Press, slept there all day, and was said to be asleep now. Back at Reidka's, the delivery boys had arrived, and, by the time Frank had unlocked, so had the two apprentices.

'We gave your letter to the chief compositor. His wife came to the door, but she fetched him and we put it into his hands.'

Frank knew Tvyordov had a wife, because she came to the dinner he gave to the whole staff and their families on his name-day. He couldn't have said exactly what she looked like, and very probably she couldn't have recognized him. There had been no answer for the apprentices to bring back from Tvyordov.

Selwyn and the number 2 and 3 compositors came in together, and, while they were still hanging up their coats downstairs, the police were announced. For this Frank blamed himself. If he'd insisted on seeing the night watchman earlier and had given him a hundred roubles — somewhere between tea-money and a bribe — Gulianin wouldn't, as he evidently had done, felt the need to take his information to the police. From them he would have got considerably less, but very likely he needed ready money immediately. Probably he was caught in the tight network of small loans, debts, repayments and foreclosures which linked the city, quarter by quarter, in its grip, as securely as the tram-lines themselves.

Frank said that he would see the police in his office. Only a captain and an orderly and to Frank's relief, in uniform. That meant the night watchman couldn't have seen Volodya leave the building, or he would have recognized from his cap that he was a student, and trouble with a student would have meant the plain clothes section, the Security. Tea was brought, the captain, though not the orderly, unbuttoned his jacket. Just a few questions, a little interrogation, a dear little interrogation. Why had Mr Reid come back here so late on the previous evening? A light in the window, who had reported that?

'My accountant, Selwyn Osipych Crane.'

The inspector smiled. 'Well, we know Selwyn Osipych.' From one end of Moscow to the other, Frank thought, when they hear Selwyn's name they either laugh or weep. In its way it was a considerable achievement. Now Selwyn himself came into the office through the connecting door, stricken and haggard. 'Frank, strange things have been happening. Ah, good-morning, officer.'

The captain looked at him indulgently. 'If you saw a light here last night, sir, that should have been reported to us at once.' He turned to Frank. 'And you, too, sir, should have reported it.'

'I left that to the night watchman,' said Frank.

'Gulianin very correctly came to us. He also heard shots.'

'Is he sure he heard them?'

The police captain stirred some jam into his tea. 'Not altogether sure. This is a very noisy street. You have a blacksmith here, and a motor-car mechanic, and up to midnight you've got the noise of the trams. Let's say he thought he heard something.'

This was a fairly strong hint that the inspector was prepared not to take things any further. He accepted a glass of vodka flavoured with caraway seeds, which was kept in the office exclusively for the police. How he could drink it so early in the morning, or indeed at all, Frank couldn't fathom. But it preserved a distinction of rank, since the orderly, knowing his place, refused it.

'Now, sir, did you find any property missing?'

'No, nothing at all.'

'Pardon me,' Selwyn broke in eagerly, 'when I came in just now I counted the first run of *Birch Tree Thoughts*. There are only seventy-four copies there. Yes, seventy-four. One has been purloined.'

'What are *Birch Tree Thoughts*?' the inspector asked.

Frank explained. In the ordinary way, poetry was suspect and, once again, might have been a matter for the Security. But this was something written by the harmless Selwyn Osipych, and the captain only said, 'Well, sir, what do birch trees think?'

Selwyn, who believed all questions should be answered, replied that they thought in the same way as women. 'Just as a woman's body, inspector, moves at her heart's promptings, so the birch tree moves in the winds of spring.'

Frank could see that the captain and the orderly were not listening, being in the genial grip of inertia and greed. He took an envelope out of his drawer, and, conscious of taking only a mild risk, since the whole unwieldly administration of All the Russias, which kept working, even if only just, depended on the passing of countless numbers of such envelopes, he slid it across the top of the desk. The inspector opened it without embarrassment, counted out the three hundred roubles it contained and transferred them to a leather container, half way between a wallet and a purse, which he kept for 'innocent income'.

'Selwyn, take the police officers downstairs and out

through the back way,' said Frank. 'They'll want, I'm sure, to have a look at the rest of the premises.'

After giving them five minutes he went to confront his No 2 and No 3 compositors, who were surrounding, like dazed mourners, Tvyordov's broken frame and scattered type and the white apron which, with its single bullet-hole hung, a victim, from its hook. The inspector could only have missed the disorder, or overlooked it, because it suited him to.

'Put the covers on,' he said.

The covers were put on the frames only on Saturday nights and on the eve of feast days. Each compositor did this for himself. The frames were sacrosanct, and the two men moved like trespassers.

Frank told them there had been an incident, a little incident, a little break-in during the night, and that he had asked Tvyordov personally not to come in today. There must have been an intruder, but he must have managed to get away. It wasn't a thief, nothing had been stolen, or nothing – Frank corrected himself – that couldn't be replaced. They were to get on with the current orders, in the first place with Muir and Merrilees' Easter catalogue, all of which had to be hand-set. This was popular with the compositors because they were paid by the page, and most of the pages were taken up with illustrations. But what had become of the open discussions, Frank asked himself, the joint decisions between management and workers which he had set his heart on when he took over Reidka's?

'The police are satisfied,' he said. 'As you've seen for yourselves, they came and they went. All we have to do is a day's work.'

But they could not adjust themselves to Tvyordov's absence. Hand-printing, whose rhythm was still that of the human body, went adrift with the disappearance of the pacesetter, assumed always to be on duty as the given condition of the whole process.

# 16

At nine o'clock, as had been arranged for his first day, the new costing accountant came to take up his duties. As Frank had told Selwyn, Aleksandr Alexsandrovich Bernov had been with Sytin's, the giant print works beyond the Sadovaya Ring. Clean-shaven, sharp-glancing, quick on the uptake, he had been impatient with his place there as head clerk, but his ideas — if they were his — were geared, perhaps irretrievably, to a large firm. He saw the business, any business, as an undeclared war against every employee below the rank of cost accountant.

Frank wanted to discuss the possibility of paying something for distributing the type, a payment compositors had been asking for, but had never been given, since the days of Gutenberg. Bernov admitted that at Sytin's, until they went over to machinery, the men used to take away the type and throw it into the river on the way home rather than distribute it in unpaid time.

'But, Frank Albertovich, I want to make this clear from the start — one mustn't encourage the survivals of the past. Hand-printing is associated now with Tolstoyans and student revolutionaries and activists in garrets and cellars. The future belongs to hot metal, of course.'

'It's still useful for small jobs and essential for fine work,' said Frank. The image persisted of Tyvordov's ruined possessions, only a few yards away, and his murdered apron. Bernov, however, urged that Reidka's should give up the small jobs altogether. Rent more warehouses, install linotype and print newspapers.

'There's a new paper or a new journal starting up every day. And with a newspaper you're printing so many identical units that you can go straight into large-scale unit costing.'

'I don't want to print newspapers,' said Frank. 'This firm has to be kept on a very delicate balance, so that it can be sold without loss and at short notice if the international situation gets worse.'

'Or if your wife, Elena Karlovna, doesn't return,' said Bernov, nodding energetically. Evidently this was discussed even at Sytin's. With quiet tact, Selwyn leaned forward.

'How do you see our future, Bernov?'

'Very simply. I'm glad you asked me. More pay for more efficiency. English and German firms have a system of merit rating for their workers. I don't know if we shall ever accept that here. But you can start by increasing the fines for drunkenness, lowering the agreed payments for waiting time when the paper runs out and so forth, and, above all, no special cases, no humanitarian allow-ances. That's what prosperity means. You're giving every-one the money they deserve.'

'But we mustn't consider what money they deserve,' said Selwyn. 'Consider only whether we, the men of business deserve to have money to give to them.'

Bernov's face, so much more expressive than was good for him, crumpled up a little.

'Of course, I'm only here as your cost accountant. Decisions are for the management only. Perhaps I ought to say, though, that the question of whether the manage-ment deserve their profits has no relevance to their econ-omic performance.'

'I'm sorry to hear you say that,' Selwyn murmured. 'Yes, truly sorry.'

Frank saw that Bernov looked bewildered, and sent out to the Bar for something to eat. *Zakuske* were brought on a covered tray by the proprietor himself, anxious to discover what kind of scandal had been reported, or not reported, by his lodger, the night watchman.

'Has he woken up?' Frank asked.

'He spoke of hearing shots when he was about his duties last night,' said the proprietor.

'Remember it's a very noisy street.'

Bernov ate rapidly and immediately began on a new proposition. At Sytin's, and perhaps during the whole of his life, he must have been deprived of proper attention.

'Look at the government expenditure this year! A hundred and ten million roubles on railways, eighty million roubles on education. Education means cheap printed books. They could be produced and even bound on the premises, using strong cartridge paper.' Frank reminded him that in times of emergency cartridge paper was liable to run very short. Bernov began to tap with a silver pencil he'd got. In 1915, the year after next, there was to be an international printing fair in Berlin, the largest in history. These industrial fairs, in his opinion, were the guarantee of continuing peace in Europe. Russia must not be outdone. The small printing shops of Moscow, places like Reid's, employing thirty to sixty people, must come to an agreement with the giants like Sytin's and prepare a joint exhibit. By that time, Frank thought, he'll have fretted himself to death.

At four o'clock two old men, two of the oldest in the place, came up to the compositors' room. They were collators, checking the order of the sheets, and seeing them, with the help of two boys and a bucket of water, through the hydraulic press. They had done the same work with the old screw press, and were never likely to do anything more difficult. Now they had an air of authority.

They had exchanged their felt slippers, which they wore at work, for leather shoes, and in these they creaked across to the ikon corner and dragged out a table to stand in front of it. A third, even older man, this time from the store room, brought in a white cloth, two candles and two tarnished silver candlesticks. They spread the cloth, adjusted the creases, crossed themselves and bowed. Frank, coming out of his office, was asked to light the candles. As he struck a match he thought uncomfortably of Volodya, who must have brought his matches with him.

The candlelight would have been more impressive if they'd turned out the electric light, but this was not important to the staff of Reidka's, who had had a service of blessing when their electricity was installed, and were proud of it. With the lighting of the candles, however, they began to come silently in, not crowding, not touching each other, and all these people who would have fought fiercely to get ahead at the tram-stop, or on the bridges watching the ice, took their stand as though their places were marked out for them. As they faced the ikon they crossed themselves, striking the forehead, each shoulder in turn, then the breast.

The men stood on the right, the tea-woman and her assistant on the left, Frank and Selwyn, as usual, in the centre. Bernov had excused himself from the ceremony, and gone home, carrying quantities of paper-work.

The whole assembly were turned to the right, with their eyes on the candles, which, like the oil for the ikon-lamp, were paid for by a voluntary weekly subscription from everyone over the age of sixteen. The ikon was not an old one. It was an example of a new photographic process which was said to be an exact simulation of oil painting, in reds and blues of excellent quality which neither time not lamp-smoke could darken, while the glittering halo of St Modestus and the letters of the alphabet in his bound book far outshone the ancient silver of the candlesticks. Those had come from the old house on the works site. Even there, Frank remembered, it had been thought unlucky to clean them.

The yardman threw the door open and the familiar heavy-treading, heavy-breathing parish priest came in, followed by a deacon and a subdeacon. From the doorway he gave his blessing. They were taken into Frank's office which, on these occasions, became a vestry. The priest came out in his stole, the deacons in their surplices. The censer was lit with a piece of red-hot charcoal from the canteen samovar. The fragrance of the smouldering cedar of Lebanon reached every corner of the room where men, women and children stood motionless.

Some of them, Frank knew, were agnostics. The store-keeper had told him that, in his opinion, soul and body were like the steam above a factory, one couldn't exist without the other. But he, too, stood motionless. The priest offered a prayer for the God-protected Tsar and his family, for the Imperial Army, that it might put down every enemy of Russia beneath its feet, for the city of Moscow and for the whole country, for those at sea, for travellers, for the sick, for the suffering, for prisoners, for the founders of the Press and the workers there, for mercy, life, peace, health, salvation, visitation, pardon and remission of sins.

Because I don't believe in this, Frank thought, that doesn't mean it's not true. He tried to call himself to order. Thomas Huxley had written that if only there was some proof of the truth of religion, humanity would clutch at it as a drowning man clutches at a hencoop. But as long as mankind doesn't pretend to believe in something they see no reason to believe, because there might be an advantage in pretending — as long as they don't do that, they won't have sunk to the lowest depths. He himself could be said to be pretending now, still more so when he had attended the Anglican chapel, with the idea of keeping Nellie company. Why he had felt alarmed when Dolly told him that her teacher said there was no God, he didn't know. The alarm suggested that as a rational being he was unsuccessful. Either that, or he had come to think of religion as something appropriate to women and children, and that would be sinking to a lower depth than Huxley had dreamed of. Perhaps, Frank thought, I have faith, even if I have no beliefs.

The priest was giving a short address. 'You are workers, and you are not only called upon to work together, but to love each other and pity each other. How can that be? You will say that you didn't choose to work next to this man or that man, he happened to be there when I first arrived, it was accidental. But remember, if that thought comes to you, that there are no accidental meetings. We never meet by chance. Either this other man, or this woman, is sent to us, or we are sent to them.'

The final blessing began. At the words 'guard this place and this house and the souls of those who dwell there' the doors opened again, and Tvyordov walked in. Every head turned towards him, and then back again. He crossed himself and went to stand in silence, with his back to his frame.

The priest held out a double-barred silver-gilt cross, the lower arm slanted to the right, representing the fates of the good and the bad thief. The congregation filed forward to kiss the cross, the men first, the two women after them. The tea-woman and her assistant kissed the priest's hands also. Although they were probably the most devout souls in the congregation, they hurried away in a state of agitation. The *pyerchestvo* for the blessing of the ikon was entirely their responsibility, and while they were upstairs the glasses might somehow have been disarranged, or supplies of small cakes and pies put out which were supposed to be kept back till later. Tyvordov also kissed the cross, but not the priest's hand.

'Go on,' Frank said to Selwyn. 'I'll be down later.'

Selwyn nodded, and escorted the priest, the deacon and the subdeacon, towards the stairs to the tea-place. They would expect to be entertained, as usual, in the office, but there was no way, at the moment, of explaining the unwelcome change in the arrangements. The congregation followed, with the exception of Tvyordov, and the room filled with that peculiar silence, as though it was stretching itself, which follows when a great number of people have recently left. Frank confronted his chief compositor.

Tvyordov did not speak to him at once. As though he was starting on his day's work, he took the covers off his frame and looked in pain, rather than in bewilderment, at the disorder. He picked up one or two letters from the violated upper case, and from habit let them fall into what would have been their right places. Then he took down his white apron, looked at the bullet-hole, put his finger through it and folded the apron neatly.

'You sent word to me not to come. But I've never missed the service of blessing.'

'You've never missed anything,' Frank replied, 'not since my father started this place, and all the work was hand-set.'

He could hardly tell Tvyordov what he hadn't told the police. He might, perhaps, have risked it if he had known what Tvyordov felt about students and about student activities, but he didn't know.

'I owe you some kind of explanation,' he began at last, 'for the state of your frame. It all happened yesterday evening.'

'It's not my frame,' replied Tvyordov, 'the frame belongs to the Press. The tools were mine, the sponge was mine, the apron was mine.'

'Anything that was damaged will be replaced.'

'That won't be necessary. What happened doesn't interest me. I shall never work in this room again. You'll have to find someone to continue instructing my apprentice, and someone to wind the clock on Saturday evenings, and clean the glass on Monday mornings. Tomorrow I shall start downstairs with the monotype.'

Onto the folded apron he put his composing stick, his setting-rule, his shears, the sponge, and the bodkin in its cork for removing wrong letters, and with two movements of his hands made them into a compact parcel. He was on his way out.

'What are you going to do with those?' Frank asked.

'I shall throw them in the river.'

# 17

Charlie's telegram said that he would arrive on the 31st of March. In Moscow that would be the 18th. The thaw would be nearly over, but the city's sealed windows hadn't yet been opened to let in the spring. Certainly he wouldn't be seeing the country at its best. Frank's hospitable instincts were disturbed. No shooting, no skating, but then Charlie didn't shoot and couldn't skate. No horse-market, but then Charlie wasn't interested in horses. The light would still be too poor for decent photography, but then he never had any luck, anyway, with his snapshots. But how would Charlie compare Moscow in springtime with Norbury, where every green front hedge and back lawn must, by now, be shooting and putting out leaves? He might think, perhaps, that Nellie never ought to have been brought to Russia.

The servants asked what must be prepared for their English visitor. Frank reminded them that he was English himself.

'Yes, but you are Russian, you are used to everything Russian,' said Toma, 'you make mistakes, and you don't mind our mistakes. God has given you patience, to take the place of your former happiness.'

'Karl Karlovich will need plenty of hot water at all times, and a boiled egg every morning.'

The 18th of March, the Feast of St Benjamin, was a general holiday. In a sense, this was convenient, as the Press would be shut, and there would be no difficulty about meeting Charlie.

'Which of us are you going to take with you to the station?' asked Dolly. 'Our uncle will expect a warm welcome.'

'I'm not taking any of you. He'll have had a tiring journey, and when he gets here he'll want a few quiet moments to take everything in.'

He was making his brother-in-law sound like a sick man, and in fact Dolly asked whether uncle Charlie was quite right in the head.

'Of course he is, but he might find it a bit confusing at first. He's never gone in for travelling. Anyway, there's nothing odd about wanting peace and quiet.'

'Is he bringing Mother back with him?' Ben asked in a perfectly level voice.

'No.'

'If Mother does come, will you have to get rid of Lisa?'

Frank knew, rather than saw, that Dolly was sitting with her head turned away, as still as if she had been frozen.

'I don't much like that expression "get rid of",' he said.

'Why not?'

What did you get rid of? Frank thought. Epidemics of cholera, draughts, mice, political opponents, bad habits. Ben had meant no harm, of course, quite the contrary. 'Get rid of' had been a favourite expression of Nellie's.

When Lisa came, a little after the rest of the household, for her weekly wages, he asked her how long she was going to stay with them.

'How can I answer that?' she said, counting her money carefully. 'I can't answer it.'

'You might say "as long as I want to".'

'It would have to be "as long as I'm wanted". That I don't need to tell you.'

Frank unlocked another drawer in the desk. 'Look, here are your papers, here's your internal passport. I'm supposed by law to keep them here, but I'm giving them back to you. You're free to go when you want to, when you need to. You can say now, "I shall stay as long as I want to." But I very much want you to stay, Lisa Ivanovna.'

Charlie, wrapped in plaids and mufflers, expected, perhaps understandably, to be taken straight from the station to Lipka Street, but Frank put the luggage in charge of a porter, and avoiding the stationmaster, whom he felt he couldn't face just at the moment, propelled Charlie into the refreshment room.

'Do they have tea here?' Charlie asked.

'Charlie, I want you to tell me about Nellie.'

'What, immediately? I haven't had much opportunity to wash, you know, since we crossed the border.'

'How's Nellie?'

Charlie sighed. 'I've got bad news for you, but no, wait, you're rushing me a bit, I haven't expressed myself rightly, there's nothing to be alarmed about. As far as I know, Nellie's perfectly well, it's only that she's not with me, she's not in Norbury.'

'You mean you've come all this way to tell me you don't know where she is?'

'She's not in material want, Frank, that I do know.'

'I should hope not. I sent off some money straight away.'

'Yes, that arrived by post, before she did. I gave it to her pretty well as soon as she arrived. I thought she was just back for a visit, you see, although I'd heard nothing from her for quite a while. She only stayed the night, stowed away her bags in the attic, where they still are, by the way, then she was off again.'

Frank ordered some tea. 'Where is she now?'

'She's school-teaching, Frank. She'd still have her cer-tificate, of course. Don't ask me where, because I don't know. I mean that she wrote me that she was at a school, and she can't be learning at her age, so she must be teaching. No address, she sent the letter poste restante to the tobacconist at the end of the road. Perhaps you remember him?'

'Can't you make the tobacconist say where it came from?'

'It wouldn't be right to persuade him to break a confidence. That's what he's paid for, really, to destroy the covering envelope. Besides, he's a Wesleyan.'

'I see.'

'I've brought her letter, if you want to look at it.'

'No, Charlie. It wasn't written to me.'

Charlie straightened himself in his chair, stirring the lemon in his tea, determined to get used to foreign customs. Well, he'll have to say it right out now, thought Frank, feeling sorry for him.

'Frank, was there any kind of disagreement between you and Nellie?'

'Did you ask her that?'

'Yes, but I didn't get an answer. She wasn't short with me, like she often used to be, I don't mean that. If I had to describe her, I'd say she was half-asleep, like a woman dreaming.'

'Did she say anything about the children?'

'I did, but she didn't.'

'What did you say?'

'I asked her what arrangements she'd made about the kiddies. She didn't answer that, either.'

'Did it strike you that, if she was like a woman half-asleep, she might have lost them?'

'No, Frank, it didn't, or I'd have been terror-struck. And after all, she hadn't lost anything else.'

Charlie had come sixteen hundred miles to give what after all, had turned out to be very little information. He had had to disturb the habits of a lifetime, take the London, Brighton & South Coast Railway into London, get his visa from the Russian consulate, change his money into marks and roubles, confront the border inspections, lose his books (*Raffles* and *Sentimental Tommy*) and his pack of patience cards, both of which had been confiscated by the customs at Verzhbolovo. 'Surely there couldn't have been much harm in a pack of cards?' Frank explained that playing cards were a state monopoly, and the proceeds went to support the Imperial Foundlings Home. 'Well, that shows the Tsar's heart is in the right place,' said Charlie.

What had propelled him, as far as Frank could make out, had been shock. He had been unsettled when Bertha died, aghast when Lloyd George had introduced National Insurance (though relieved when it turned out that there wouldn't be pensions for criminals), worried – as he had told Frank – by the recent behaviour of Englishwomen and English railwaymen and printers, but none of these had constituted the kind of distress that Nellie had caused him when, supposed to be in Moscow, she had rung the bell at Longfellow Road, and worse still, disappeared the next day. Perhaps, too, there was a wish, long unrecognized, to go one better than his much-travelled sister. Who would have believed that Charlie Cooper would ever get as far as Russia? But there was no practical object in his journey whatever. The only idea that had come to him, he said, was that 'they might advertise'. Frank pointed out that advertisements were for lost and missing persons, and Nellie, properly speaking, was neither. Charlie, however, had been thinking of something on the lines of the Lost Boys in *Peter Pan*, who appealed to their mothers to come home. Frank was rather surprised at this stroke of imagination, but Charlie said it had been suggested by the vicar.

'So you've been discussing my troubles quite extensively in Norbury.'

'Not extensively, Frank. Only to sympathetic ears.'

Once they were back in Lipka Street, Charlie explained that he intended to stay about a week or ten days, to see whatever there was to be seen, and to broaden his mind a bit, because that was what travel was for. He'd been afraid that it might be inconvenient, but he could see that he needn't have worried about that – Frank was very well able to manage, and the whole place, he could also see, was something like. The warmth of a Russian household and the excitement of the servants' greeting to a distinguished relative from a foreign country powerfully affected him, so that he was much less like a man on an awkward and distressing mission than a tripper on a day-outing.

'My word, Frank, you don't do yourself badly. Plenty of everything, people to look after you, the house kept warm all the time, almost too warm for comfort, I'd say. I can't call to mind a single house in Norbury with anything more than coal fires.'

'I should be careful of the vodka if I were you, Uncle Charlie,' said Ben anxiously. 'It doesn't taste of anything but it's quite strong.'

'Uncle Charlie needs something quite strong,' said Dolly.

'Well, I'll take a little,' Charlie said amiably, 'if your father thinks it's good for me.'

'It's not at all good for you,' said Frank. But the vodka, pliant, subtle, and fiery, eased the moment, as it had done for so many millions of others.

Charlie was not deaf, but he didn't always entirely take in what was said to him. In this way, although he was sometimes taken off guard, he was spared a good deal. He helped himself freely at table, remarking, 'I hope I'm not overdoing it.'

'You can't overdo it,' said Frank, 'the cook will be disappointed if you don't take plenty.'

'She needn't worry. It's excellent, and then there's all these little touches, these slices of cucumber, I mean, that's what I call little touches. I'd never have believed that the housekeeping would go ahead like this while you were managing on your own, so to speak.'

'He isn't managing on his own,' said Dolly. 'He has Lisa.'

'There's a Russian girl who looks after the children,' said Frank. 'I don't know why she isn't here now.' He had expected her to be there, and although she was presumably only a few yards away he was not able to prevent himself from feeling the deprivation as a physical pain.

'You were a very long time at the station,' Dolly said. 'Lisa had supper upstairs with Annushka.'

'Well, I hope I shall meet your Miss Lisa tomorrow, then,' said Charlie. 'A good thing she's got an English name, isn't it? Just for a chat, then tomorrow.'

'I'm afraid Lisa won't be able to chat to you,' said Dolly. 'She doesn't know any English.'

'Dear me, that's a pity. You'll have to see if you can teach her any. Just "how do you do?" and "thank you" and "A was an apple-pie" – just useful phrases to be going on with.'

Dolly and Ben both left the room.

'They're unusual kiddies,' said Charlie. 'They've got a quaint way with them. You can't tell what's going on in a child's mind, of course. Those two join in the conversation quite freely, but that doesn't mean you can tell what they're thinking. I'm not sure that Nellie and me were ever permitted to join in quite as freely as that. There was rather rigid discipline in our home, you see.'

The tea came in, and Toma, who wanted a closer look at the brother-in-law, took up once again with Frank a grievance of long standing about the necessity of buying a fifth samovar. One was upstairs now with Lisa Ivanovna and the two large ones were in the kitchen. The argument was not a formality and went on for some time, while Charlie sat perspiring in the warmth of the room, turning his head from one unintelligible speaker to the other. The door, meanwhile was left open, and Lisa came in.

Charlie got to his feet, was introduced as Karl Karlovich, and could only smile. Lisa also smiled, and said to Frank in Russian, 'Please don't think I intended to sit down here. I know you want to talk to your brother-in-law.'

'No, I don't want to talk to him,' Frank answered in English. 'Stay here, I'm in love with you.'

'Pardon, I didn't quite catch that,' said Charlie.

Lisa went silently away.

'She looks like a very refined type of young lady, Frank. A pity she's had her hair cut short, as it's quite a nice colour. At home I'd have thought she was a suffragist.'

'She's employed here on a temporary basis,' said Frank. 'I mean while Nellie's away.'

'Oh, I see, she's not a young lady, she's a young woman.'

'I'm sure her hair will grow again quite quickly,' said Frank.

# 18

Charlie continued to show an unexpected readiness to enjoy himself. This began, conventionally enough, with a call at the Chaplaincy, where Frank himself, since the departure of Miss Kinsman, had felt himself coldly received. If this was so, Charlie didn't notice it. He repeated to Mrs Graham his amazement at the house-keeping at 22 Lipka Street.

'That's Russia, I suppose. You'll feel the difference, you and your husband, when you come to the end of your ministry here and go back home again. I tell Frank that in his house it's more like the Arabian nights.'

'I'm glad, Frank,' said Mrs Graham, lighting one of her horrible cigarettes, 'that your house has become like something out of the Arabian nights.'

'Someone to open the door,' Charlie went on, 'some-one to shut it for you, someone to bring anything you're in want of. With a smile, you know! And then the kiddies are no trouble at all.'

'Ah yes,' said Mrs Graham. 'I heard that Frank had engaged a girl to look after them.'

'Of course, when she does say anything it's in Russian and I can't make head or tail of it,' said Charlie. 'But you've only got to look at her to see that she's the right sort. She's "just the sort of creature that Nature did intend". Do you know that song, Mrs Graham?'

'No, I don't,' said Mrs Graham, afraid, perhaps, that Frank's brother-in-law might begin to sing.

'It's an Irish song,' he told her. 'It's called "I met her in the garden where the praties grow." But you can't draw a hard and fast line between the nationalities. It describes her to a T.'

'Lisa used to work as an assistant in Muir and Merrilees,' said Frank. 'I hope –'

'In which department?'

'The men's handkerchiefs, I think.'

'Ah, yes.'

'I hope that when you and the Chaplain next come to see us, you'll have a talk with her.'

'Oh, you mustn't trouble yourself about invitations,' said Mrs Graham, 'until your wife comes back.'

Mrs Graham struck Charlie as a gracious, friendly woman, who seemed to have a kind word for everyone. He was also impressed by Selwyn, a clever chap, he thought, who'd read a lot. He was surprised that Nellie hadn't mentioned him more in her letters home.

'He told me he was a poet, Frank. I wonder if you knew that?'

'Yes, I did know it.'

'And he's a vegetarian, too, like George Bernard Shaw. But Shaw isn't a poet. It must be easier for him, writing prose, to sustain himself on vegetables.'

'Selwyn doesn't eat much at any time,' said Frank.

'It seems an odd thing for a management accountant. But you can't argue with genius, it strikes where it will. When he took me yesterday to hear that pianist, you know, Scriabin, yes, at that concert hall, and we were walking back together, he suddenly told me to stop, and we stopped dead in the middle of the tram-lines.'

'What for?'

'He didn't give any reason. He just threw back his head and looked at the stars, and we moved on almost immediately.'

Selwyn had also given Charlie a copy of *Birch Tree Thoughts*. There it was, in its familiar buff paper cover. 'It would have been more of a keepsake, of course, if it had been in Russian, but then, if it hadn't been in English I shouldn't have been able to follow it. I've had a glance through it. This one is a kind of lullaby, I think, to make a child drop off to sleep. I didn't know Crane was a married man.'

'It isn't the poet speaking,' said Frank. 'If I'm thinking of the right one. It's a birch tree.'

'Well, I consider it a privilege to meet a poet on equal terms like that. You must feel it too, in the day-to-day running of the business.'

While Selwyn and Charlie had been at the conservatoire Frank had taken the opportunity to call on Mrs Graham again. He had telephoned to ask her if he could have another word with her; it hadn't been possible, he said, the other evening, but at the moment his brother-in-law was out.

There was no one else in the drawing room, evidently she'd thought it worth while to keep it clear for him. He began at once, 'I wanted to ask you if you'd heard from Miss Kinsman. To tell you the truth, I haven't been altogether easy about her.'

'Did you expect to be?' asked Mrs Graham.

'I'm not sure that I have any special responsibility towards her. But I know that she'd lost her job and needed another one, and perhaps she expected . . . I mean that if she was disappointed, I'm very sorry.'

'Ah, but are you?' Mrs Graham said. 'Would you consider me old-fashioned to an absurd degree if I said that a man's duty to a woman, even an older woman, or perhaps I should say particularly to an older woman, in a strange city, is to escort her safely to wherever she happens to want to go?'

'No, I don't think you're old-fashioned, Mrs Graham. I find you confusing, but that's a different matter. I find all women confusing, even Dolly. It's because you use a different manner, if I may put it that way, according to who you're with. Now your husband would never do that.'

'He should be able to, it was part of his pastoral training,' said Mrs Graham briskly. 'I admit I didn't need training in it myself. But in any case, you didn't find poor Muriel Kinsman confusing?'

'Yes, I did. But even so, I wasn't sufficiently polite to her, or even reasonable.'

'Well, she arrived safely at Harwich. She was completely harmless, or as harmless as a penniless person can be. The poor always cause trouble, my father was a country curate and we were poor as dirt. Where did she go? Well, I gave her a note to the Distressed Gentlewomen, and Mr Crane knew of a Tolstoyan settlement somewhere near London, with running water, of course. But that isn't really what you came here to talk about, is it? My husband wouldn't have been able to advise you, because it wouldn't have been his business. It isn't my business either, but then I don't care whether it is or not.'

'I haven't any secrets,' said Frank. 'Everyone in Moscow knows everything I do.'

'Perhaps you've been in Moscow too long.'

'I hope not.'

'I won't say "let's get to the point". We arrived there

a long time ago. This young woman. She, also, was recommended by the great recommender, Mr Crane. He's an idealist. I don't accuse him of anything worse than that. He's not of the earth, earthy, he's of the clouds, cloudy. But what does your brother-in-law think?'

'Charlie thinks very highly of Lisa Ivanovna,' said Frank. 'He's told you that already.'

'Of course he thinks quite highly of her!' Mrs Graham cried, raising her voice to a pitch that Frank had never heard before. 'Show me a single man in this city who wouldn't! Quiet, blonde, slow-witted, nubile, docile, doesn't speak English, hardly speaks at all in fact, sloping shoulders, half-shut eyes, hasn't broadened out yet though I daresay she will, proper humility, reasonable manners, learned I suppose behind the counter at Muirka's.'

'I don't think her eyes are usually half-shut,' said Frank.

'You're all of you serf-owners at heart! Yes, this brother-in-law too! Fifty years after Emancipation, and you're still chasing them into the straw-stacks!'

'Don't let yourself be carried away, Mrs Graham,' said Frank. 'They've never had serfs in Norbury.'

'Still you haven't answered what I asked you. The brother-in-law. Over here, presumably, in distress at his sister's disappearance. What does he think of the situation he finds in your house?'

'There's nothing to think. If Lisa had come to work for us, and Nellie had left the house in consequence, there might have been some objection, but it was quite the other way about.'

'Yes, quite, quite the other way about,' said Mrs Graham hoarsely. She blew out quantities of smoke. Frank felt dismayed.

'You're distressing yourself unnecessarily. I'm sorry it should be on my account.'

'Do I irritate you?' Mrs Graham asked, gallantly trying to regain her usual manner.

'Not yet.'

'There's something else. I find your Lisa difficult to place. We were saying that Selwyn Crane is an idealist, by which we meant, or at least I did, that he's easily taken in. How much did he know about her? I'd say she was probably a deacon's daughter, or a psalm-singer's, or a bell-ringer's – some church official, anyway.'

'I think her father was a joiner.'

'You've seen her documents, of course.'

'Of course.'

'I'm only asking you the questions you ought to have asked yourself. Very likely you have. After all, you were brought up here. You must see a lot of young Russians, a lot of students, but after all Russians can be young without being students – many more of them, I mean, than we do here at the Chaplaincy. A joiner's daughter!

Well, I don't know that I've ever spoken to a joiner. Milkmen, sewingwomen, photographers — terrible people! — German dentists — but not joiners. I'm glad to say that so far the woodwork at the Chaplaincy has held up, and there's been no need to call a joiner in.'

'We were talking about Lisa Ivanovna,' said Frank.

'Well, let me put it quite plainly. Perhaps I'm quite on the wrong tack in thinking there's anything mysterious about her. But do you think it's possible that she's connected with any kind of revolutionary group?'

'Mrs Graham, what I think is this: your imagination's running away with you a little. I can't help feeling that you're determined to find something wrong with Lisa, however unlikely. Politics need spare time, and anyone who looks after my three children for twenty-four hours of the day and night won't have much spare time left.'

'But, my dear Frank,' said Mrs Graham, leaning forward, 'is she sleeping in the house?'

It was the first time she had ever called him 'my dear'. He went on rapidly, 'and then, political activity needs a certain temperament, I think. For example, Dolly's teacher —'

'Oh, the godless one!' said Mrs Graham. 'Yes, I've heard of *her*. But I'm sure you need have no fears about Dolly. Never did I meet a child of her age whose head was screwed on more firmly.'

Frank wondered exactly what Dolly had been saying

when she came to tea, as she sometimes did, at the Chaplaincy. Mrs Graham rolled another handful of rank shag, and squared her thin shoulders. She's going to pieces, Frank thought. 'No hard feelings,' he said, and in her contempt for such a commonplace remark, she began to feel better, so that they parted almost on friendly terms.

# 19

'Your wife and her brother must be close, very close!' exclaimed Mrs Kuriatin.

'I don't think so,' said Frank. 'They haven't seen each other for some years.'

'No tie is as strong as that between a brother and a sister, none. Only prison and hunger are stronger, that's what's said. What do I know of what Arkady is doing? But I know what's in the heart of all my six brothers in Smolensk.'

Kuriatin, too, seemed extravagantly delighted at the arrival of the brother-in-law, whom he insisted as regarding as a lawyer, perhaps as a public prosecutor from an important district. 'Norbury. What is the significance of that in Russian?'

'Northern city, I suppose,' said Frank doubtfully.

'The same meaning, then, as Peking,' said Kuriatin in triumph.

He must show, he said, this newcomer how a Russian enjoys himself, in a way quite unknown to the West. Ordinarily he would have done this by taking a taxi to

THE BEGINNING OF SPRING

the gipsy brothels in Petrovsky Park. Were there good gipsy brothels in Norbury? Frank reassured him on this point. But these places were all compulsorily shut during Lent, and Frank stipulated that Charlie who, after all, was musical, shouldn't be taken to Rusalochka's. The motor-car, then. They could go in Kuriatin's Wolseley Star – a 50 h.p. model, with detachable wheels, which Frank felt was a wise precaution – to, let's say, the Merchants' Church, between Kursk and Ryazan, about twelve miles out of Moscow. The roads, though, were still covered with only half-melted snow.

'No matter, I have Columbus tyres from Provodnik's. Provodnik sells only the best, and makes me a special price. They will go over any road, and in the worst weather.' Ben confirmed this, although Mikhailo, Kuriatin's chauffeur, promoted from head groom, had never let him get a proper look at the engine and hadn't, Ben thought, really got the proper hang of it himself.

Kuriatin was in high spirits. He knew Charlie couldn't understand anything he said, but treated this as a jest, to be overcome by noise and persistence. 'You'll come back deaf,' Frank said. 'I shall be responsible for you to Nellie, you know.' He told Bernov, who as part of his own plans for advancement had taken a course in commercial English, that he'd have to go along as interpreter.

'You surprise me, Frank Albertovich. A day's work at the Press will be lost if I go on this expedition, and if they want to attend Vespers at the monastery we shall have to stay the night.'

'You won't get as far as that.'

'You anticipate a breakdown?'

'If that happens, get Mikhailo to check the carburettor. This Russian petrol is very low on benzine.'

'What is a carburettor? I wish you were coming with us,' said Bernov, and Frank felt a surge of affection for him, which was replaced when he got to work by remorse. Reidka's had settled down at once into its new arrangement, giving him an indescribable sense of quietened anxiety and present satisfaction, such as he had had as a small boy when watching a bee-hive or a top. During the day, new official regulations arrived, requiring that hence forward all fines for absence or drunkenness should not be held back by the firms concerned, but should be paid into an account under government control, where the Ministry of the Interior would decide, eventually, how the money could best be spent for the benefit of the workers. The fines didn't amount to much, but Frank knew that Bernov would have enjoyed deciding whether the small amount of lost income was an overhead, a variable cost or an abnormal cost. Anxious detail was a relief to him from the large-scale schemes which he was already beginning to see would never, alas, find a place at Reidka's. And now, instead of a day of delicious close evaluation and adjustment, he had to rattle, in deep

embarrassment, through the chilly landscape on Kuriatin's outing. But Frank knew he couldn't have asked
Selwyn to go. Although Kuriatin's change of heart hadn't
lasted long, only, indeed, until the next working day,
there was no knowing when, in Selwyn's presence, it
might return, and Frank couldn't see how a change of
heart would fit in to a day out in the Wolseley.

He was late home, having helped to read over the
proofs of *Three Men in a Boat*. He had something to eat, of
sorts, in Markel's Bar. When he got back, Lisa brought
in the children to say good-night, something which had
never happened to him before, and which he thought
only happened in other families. It was most unusual,
to begin with, for them all to agree to go to bed at the
same time.

'Is Uncle Charlie back?' asked Dolly

'No, he isn't back yet.'

'Do you think they've had a puncture?'

'Very likely,' said Frank. 'All cars have punctures.'

'They ought to make them all with solid wheels, like
Trojans.'

'Perhaps, but people want to be comfortable.'

'I don't see that Uncle Charlie ought to stay here
much longer,' said Dolly. 'He hasn't brought Mother
back with him, and he can't tell us when she's coming,
either.'

'Don't you care anything about your uncle?' asked

Frank, with a straightforward desire for information. Annushka, born to take life in the way easiest to herself and to extract from any situation only the aspect which did her most credit, shouted, 'I love my Uncle Charlie!'

'He seems to like everything so much,' said Ben, trying to render justice, 'we're not used to that.'

'And his visit hasn't led to anything,' said Dolly. 'He isn't supposed to be here just to enjoy himself.'

Frank pointed out that Charlie's train tickets to London, via Warsaw and Berlin, were booked for the 28th of March, Russian calendar, and it was the family's business to see that he enjoyed himself till then. He would rather have liked Dolly to give him a hug, but she had apparently decided against this. All day, ever since he could remember, Frank had been used, in Moscow, to physical human warmth, and not only when he was a child. Even now, his Russian business contacts frequently threw their arms round him, so did his servants and his employees, while the tea-woman and the yardman, if he didn't manage to stop them, kissed his hands. All that Dolly gave him was a fearless, affectionate glance.

Frank sent all the servants to bed and said that he would sit up for Karl Karlovich himself. At half-past ten Kuriatin and his party came back, not in the Wolseley, which had started to pour out smoke and had been abandoned, with Mikhailo, a few miles out of Moscow, but in a broken-down horse and carriage which was all they'd been able to hire on the spot. Kuriatin was noisy and anxious to show that everything had been a success, Bernov looked tired, shrunken and sober, Charlie was his usual self. He saw nothing amiss with their day. He hadn't, he explained, taken any vodka as he thought it might be affecting his bowels, but he had had a few glasses of kvass, the Russian beer made, they told him, out of bread, which was just as remarkable, when you came to think of it, as if they'd made bread out of beer. Clever people, the Russians. It didn't matter that they'd never reached the church. When you'd seen one Orthodox church, you'd seen them all. And at the traktir they'd had a special dish, a fish-pie with a hole in the top, into which you crammed caviare.

'Mr Kuriatin's treated me very liberally all day,' he went on. 'I'm beginning to see that over here the expression "friend of the family" means just what it says.'

'So it does in England,' said Frank.

'I shouldn't have understood, of course, without Mr Bernov here, and his useful gift of tongues. He was explaining to me on the way back what Mr Kuriatin was saying, I mean about how much he felt for you and how he'd like to do something more for you.'

Kuriatin, who had caught his name, nodded, laughed, rolled his eyes and emitted sounds, though not quite at the same time. He was like a mechanical figure in a secondhand toy shop, slightly out of kilter.

'He wants to take the three children into his household, Frank, for as long as need be, so that you'd be free of all responsibility. What do you think of that? It seems his wife is a motherly soul who can't have too many kiddies in the house. And it wouldn't cost you anything. He held out his arms wide, just like he's doing now, and said, "Let them regard me as their second father." Didn't he, Mr Bernov?'

'Yes,' said Bernov. 'He repeated that more than once.'

'What's he saying now?' asked Charlie.

'He's saying that a man who has drunk vodka is like a child: what is in his heart comes straight to his lips.'

'Is that a traditional saying?'

'It may be,' said Bernov, 'I've never lived in a village and I'm not familiar with traditional sayings.'

'It doesn't matter anyway,' said Frank. 'He doesn't really want to adopt my children. It's just a general expression of good-will, or more likely the opposite.'

'Surely, as a business man, he'll be as good as his word!' Charlie cried. 'Surely he's the soul of hospitality.'

'Of course he is.'

Suddenly bored, Kuriatin got off the sofa with a plunging motion and, not waiting for the samovar, made his way out, yelling for his coat and boots. The carriage had been kept waiting in the drizzle. He drove off, without offering Bernov a lift.

'It's of no importance, Frank Albertovich, I'd prefer to

take a tram in any case.' Bernov struggled into his galoshes. 'This time, however, you've asked too much of me. I'm your cost accountant and I should prefer to confine myself to my daily duties.'

Charlie was tired and went straight to bed, still praising and approving. This damp weather was so much healthier than a hot, dry climate. A good thing, really, that the Wolseley had broken down, because up to then it had seemed to make Mr Bernov a bit unwell. But Mr Kuriatin had known what to do, and at the traktir he'd made him take a special remedy, a draught of mothballs dissolved in vodka.

'It's a useful tip, really. One ought to write all these things down somewhere handy. Well, Frank, I'll say goodnight.'

# 20

It seemed, on the day before Charlie was due to leave, as though he had been there for as long as they could remember. He had taken to eating kasha, two or even three bowls of it, at breakfast, with a lump of butter in each. 'I shan't get this at home,' he said. He had, he felt, got a pretty good general look at Russia. On his drive with Kuriatin and Bernov he hadn't been far out of the city, but far enough, he thought, to see what the rest of the country and its agriculture must be like.

'I saw cabbage stumps everywhere. There's too much reliance on the cabbage in Russia, Frank. If I have any criticism, it's that these people aren't like our allotment-holders at home. A farm or a factory can make a loss, but an English allotment, never. And that brings me to my other point.'

The other point had to be left for the time being, because it was a fixed principle in Norbury that nothing of importance must be discussed in front of the servants.

'Even though they don't understand me they might gather the sense of my gestures and facial expressions. You don't want them to know your business.'

'Everyone knows my business,' said Frank.

Charlie walked with him as far as the tram-stop. 'I'm sorry I haven't seen your place of work. But I daresay a rest will do me no harm. And Dolly has promised to come with me to the Rows after school and interpret for me to the shopkeepers, so that I can get a few little presents to take back home. Now, that brings me to the point I was unable to make at breakfast.'

'What was that?'

'It's about the kiddies. That offer of Kuriatin's — there's a rough diamond for you, if you like — it set me thinking. You turned that down, but how does this strike you — suppose I were to take the three of them with me tomorrow when I go back to England?'

'Look, Charlie —'

'I've surprised you, haven't I, Frank? But it's a grief to me that your kiddies don't know their native land. We were talking about allotments — well, they've none of them ever seen one. I daresay they've never even seen a vegetable marrow. And then, you know, I find it a bit lonely in the house at times.'

'You want them to live with you permanently?'

'Think it over, Frank. I know you're not having an easy time, even if we haven't talked much about it. Think it over during the day, and see how it appeals to you.'

★    ★    ★

'Your father looked quite put out,' Charlie said to Dolly, as they walked into the Trading Rows. 'I hope I didn't speak out of turn.'

'Don't worry about it now,' Dolly told him. She was in tearing spirits, wearing her new fur-lined overcoat over her school uniform, and totally in charge. 'We'll get your presents first. Then you can give me some tea, and I'll tell you what I think.'

They climbed to the Upper Rows, the top storey of the great market, intersected in each direction by glass-covered corridors from which the moving mass of shoppers, also under glass, could be seen swarming forth and back. The middle storey was for wholesale. Upstairs, they faced half a mile of merchandise, laid out for ready spenders. Dolly's eyes shone.

'Just a few items,' said Charlie feebly. 'There are neighbours who've been good to me, there's the vicarage, and I suppose the Choral Society and one or two people at work.'

'What are you taking back for Mother?'

'I'm not sure of her whereabouts, Dolly dear. Otherwise, you know, I should have –'

Taking his list away from him, Dolly dragged him rapidly forward. 'This is the grocery section. Not the imported groceries, the Russian things. Tinned Sturgeon in wine, potted elk, dried elk, caviare of course, but this isn't the best kind, partridges in brandy. Then down this way there's the *galanterya*, amber beads, kid gloves, silk fans with pearl handles, velvet babies' boots, all that sort of thing, or you can get peasants' feast day dresses, you don't have to buy the whole dress, you can just get a *kokosnik* or a *shugai*. Now we're getting on to the gold and silver and jewellery and the religious objects.'

'I can't afford these things, Dolly. Can't we take a short cut? In any case, they wouldn't do for presents, religious objects would look quite out of place at the vicarage.'

'They've got pearl ear-rings here. They're only river pearls, though.'

As she spoke she turned her head towards him. Charlie was taken aback to see, what he'd never noticed before, that her ears were pierced in an altogether foreign way, and that she was wearing a pair of gold sleepers.

'When did you have that done, dear?'

'Oh, when I was two weeks old, I suppose. Annushka's are just the same.'

He said awkwardly. 'Perhaps you'd like me to get you some of these pearls, then?' Dolly laughed. 'I've got plenty of them at home. We're not allowed to wear them at school.'

Taking pity on him, she turned left at the crossing point of the next glass corridors, and they bought a number of small birchwood objects and a cigar-case. She counted his change and recovered, without argument, another thirty kopeks. Charlie had to be careful with his purchases, all of them wrapped by now in coarse paper, or, said Dolly, they might break.

To get a glass of tea, they had to go down to the restaurant, which was in the basement of one of the sandstone towers of the Rows. But the place was dismayingly full, the air thick as gas and thronged with customers' elbows on the shove.

'We won't stay here, we'll go and have tea with Selwyn Osipych.'

'I don't know where he lives, Dolly, and surely he'll be working at the Press.'

'No, he won't. My father goes in every day, except some times not on Saturday. Selwyn doesn't go in on Thursdays. They're both in on Fridays because it's pay-day. No one's allowed by law to be paid on Saturdays or the eve of feast-days, to stop them getting drunk the next morning.'

'That's all very well, but it may not be very convenient to call if he's not expecting us,' Charlie pleaded.

Selwyn lived in the east Miasnitskaya, just where it changed from a prosperous to a doubtful quarter. One street further and you were among the brothels, male and female, the Khitrovo market which was not much like the shops in the Rows, and the lodging houses where job-seekers, cholera suspects, military deserters and wanted criminals hid themselves by day. Dolly would not, in the ordinary way of things, have been allowed so far to the east of the Miasnitskaya. But she knew the house, and brazenly rang for the doorman.

'See if Selwyn Osipych is at home.'

'He has rooms in this house, but he is scarcely ever here.' Selwyn, however, came down himself to greet them.

'You should have told me —'

'I know,' said Charlie. 'But I'm not at the helm this afternoon. We couldn't get tea at the Rows.' Behind the other two on the stairs, he persevered with his explanation. 'Well, you're both of you very welcome,' Selwyn insisted. Dolly raced up first. Selwyn's room was lit only with paraffin lamps and the red glow of the stove.

'I don't have electricity here,' he said, 'or tea, I mean tea as such. I make an infusion of the nine herbs of healing — buttercup, rattray, marguerite, dead nettle, wild parsley, St John's Wort, clover, balsam and grass. I gather them in summertime, and dry them out on my return.'

'Those herbs of healing are for sick cows,' said Dolly.

'Healing knows no barriers, Dolly.'

'Dead nettles, ugh! Send the doorman out for some tea and a lemon.'

The doorman, however, was at the ready to sell some of his own supply. Indeed, he'd got it out as soon as he saw that Selwyn Osipych had visitors. Few wanted to drink an infusion of the nine herbs. Charlie felt that perhaps they were being difficult guests, and said that the grass and buttercup mixture sounded very interesting, and he'd been recommended something like that for asthma.

'Each plant is under the patronage of a different saint,' said Selwyn. 'These things aren't purely medicinal.'

The room had a ceiling of carved wood, which repeated the pattern of the gables. It was painted white, and Selwyn had got a carpenter to put up row after row of book-shelves, which held not only his books but his shoe-making tools, his needle and thread and his jars of herbs. The same carpenter had made the plain wooden chairs and table, jointed without a single nail. Charlie looked round for something to praise, but was reduced to, 'Nice place you've got here.'

'I'm not sure that it's nice,' said Selwyn, quietly. 'I looked for somewhere to live here because it's on the edge of the Khitrovo market.'

'Is that a good place to shop?'

'Yes, if you want to find whatever's been stolen from you during the last six months, or have yourself tattooed, or get an abortion.'

Charlie frowned, glancing towards Dolly. 'Say no more. I suppose the rent is pretty reasonable, then.'

'Selwyn Osipych doesn't mind so much about the rent,' said Dolly. 'He lives here because he likes to walk about at night among the unfortunate.'

'It's quite true that I don't need much sleep,' Selwyn said. 'And there are times late at night when the souls of men and women open naturally, as is the case with certain plants.'

'Shall I put on the kettle?' Dolly asked. Selwyn had one of the very few kettles in Moscow. There was no word in Russian for it. He had brought it back several years ago from a visit to his home town, Tunbridge Wells.

'You don't have all these servants, then?' asked Charlie.

'No, the relationship seems to me a false one.'

'Well, our Dolly seems to be very handy in the kitchen.' Selwyn explained to him what Tolstoy had told him; if grown men and women live simply, and do tasks of which the need is obvious, the children will soon wish to share them.

'Do you think Nellie lived simply?' Charlie asked.

After Dolly had seen to the tea she sat down and said abruptly: 'Uncle Charlie wants to take us back with him to Norbury. How he got such an idea into his head I can't think.'

'Now, my dear,' said Charlie, 'you're speaking more sharply than you intend, I'm sure. I made the offer to your father, as I told you, in all good faith. I was only surprised that it upset him so much.'

'I think I understand it,' said Selwyn leaning forward, all interest and concern. 'Dolly doesn't want to leave her father.'

'We don't want to leave Russia,' said Dolly. 'It's the beginning of spring. We want to go to the dacha.'

Sucking the last slice of lemon, sitting in the tender lamplight, she looked at them tolerantly.

'We don't want to leave Lisa Ivanovna.'

# 21

That evening Charlie, to Frank's amazement, repeated his offer.

'You're not going to start on about that again?'

'Yes, Frank, I am, because it's come to me that you were against the whole idea because you thought I wouldn't be able to manage on my own on the journey, and it's true, I haven't much experience of looking after kiddies. But now I can see a way round that, and it'll have another benefit too, because I mentioned to you that I was rather lonely at times in Longfellow Road. Now how would it be if I got Miss Lisa to come with me? I mean at the same wages you're paying her here, which I take it are fair ones.'

Frank stared at him, but saw that he was obliged to believe him. 'I don't know, Charlie,' he said. 'How would it be? Have you asked her?'

'You're forgetting that I can't make myself understood in Russian. The thing, naturally, would be for you to speak to her on my behalf.'

In silence, Frank set himself to compose a short speech.

'Dear Lisa, please consider the following three possibilities, which I've been asked to put before you by my brother-in-law. First, Karl Karlovich wants you, although he doesn't know it himself. He would like you to go to England with him to look after the children on the journey, at the same wages I pay you (which he takes it are fair ones), and then later, when he realizes what he really feels, to go to bed with him, to the disgust, disapproval, and envy of all his neighbours in Norbury. Second possibility: Karl Karlovich wants you, &c. &c., but he's sharper than I thought, and he *does* know it himself. The results would be the same, and at the same wages I pay you, (which he takes it are fair ones), but would take place a good deal sooner. A third possibility: Karl Karlovich doesn't want you, but he suspects that I do. This distresses him, partly on his sister's account, partly, I think, on mine, as I'm sure he has my moral welfare at heart, and it's come to him that if he can get you away to England (still at the same wages), he'll deliver me from temptation.'

'I don't quite know how I'd explain it to her,' he said aloud. 'But are you sure the children want to go to Norbury?'

Charlie looked disheartened. 'Not quite sure,' he said.

Frank decided that after all his brother-in-law was a more honourable man than himself, but he also realized that he didn't care, and the relief of admitting this combined, to some extent, with the relief of seeing Charlie off with his hold-all, his portmanteau, the presents which he had bought with Dolly in the Rows and the dozen bottles of vodka and fifty cakes of green tea which Kuriatin, at the last moment, had sent to the station. Although it was only ten days since he'd arrived, Charlie seemed largely to have forgotten the practical details of the journey. Customs regulations, time zones, warning bells, were all scattered in his mind, all muddled. Certainly he seemed to have forgotten the main object of his visit. Nellie wasn't mentioned between them.

'I'll let you know when I get back safely, Frank, you can count on that. I feel I haven't thanked you half enough. And I'm more than sorry if I've caused any unpleasantness by suggesting ... I mean, if you think there's any kind of cloud between us, I'm quite prepared to tear up the return half of my ticket here and now and go straight back to Lipka Street with you.'

To emphasize what he meant he took out his wallet, but the return ticket was not there. A search followed, Frank going through Charlie's coat, feeling like an amateur pick-pocket, and finding the ticket at last, after all, in the wallet. The third bell rang. Charlie clambered up the high steps of the carriage and, as the train moved out of the station, tried to look back out of the window, but too many of the other passengers crowded in front of him and he was lost to sight.

\*     \*     \*

'Has he gone?' asked Dolly.

The same room, the same soup, the same bread, but no Charlie. It seemed as they all sat down together, as though a threat had been removed. The day settled down, once again, without a ripple. Lisa still chewed energetically, and still spoke only when she was spoken to, she still created a sense of repose without tedium, as though the natural condition of life was peace. I've got to disturb her, Frank thought, at all costs.

'I don't think I shall ever get married,' Dolly went on. 'Lisa, too, probably won't ever get married.'

'Lisa, why did you tell Dolly that?' Frank asked.

'What I told her was that once, perhaps even ten years ago, it was considered a terrible thing in the villages for a woman to be single.'

'That's not the same thing at all.'

'No, not the same.'

'My teacher isn't married,' said Dolly. 'Miss Kinsman wasn't married.'

'None of you children ever met Miss Kinsman,' said Frank. 'I didn't know you'd ever heard of her. Lisa, I give you my permission to reprove Dolly if she oppresses me, as all women, without exception, seem to be impelled to do.'

'Why is it better now for women than it was ten years ago?' asked Ben.

'It is better,' said Frank. 'But perhaps Lisa would explain why.'

Lisa never changed colour, but now she put down her spoon and said, 'I haven't much practice in explaining. It's unkind to ask anyone for more than they have to give.'

'Unkind!' said Frank, aghast.

Next day, at Reidka's, as soon as Bernov was out of the way, he asked Selwyn whether he'd ever thought of him as an unkind or inhuman person. While Selwyn, instead of denying it immediately, was thinking the question over in his gentle, irritating way, Frank said, 'You told me it was my duty to try to understand Lisa Ivanovna.'

'I don't know that I used the word "duty",' said Selwyn, recalled to himself. 'That necessarily suggests something that you don't want to do. I envisaged a moment somewhat like entering the warmest room of the bath house, the steam room, where desire and duty become one. Do you follow me?'

'Quite well, as a matter of fact,' said Frank. 'But the trouble is that I can't do much when there's so little time. I only see her in the morning and again in the evening.'

'That's more, to be honest with you, than I should have expected. I don't think you ought to reproach yourself on that score. It's possible, though, that Lisa Ivanovna's life is, to some extent, joyless. If that is so, I'm quite prepared to take her out some evening, as I did your brother-in-law. All large meetings are banned, of course, particularly for young people, but we might try a Temperance group, or a gathering of the Russian Pilgrims of the Way of Humility, or a literary circle. All these events are free, or cost very little, and all, as long as the numbers are kept small, are approved by the political police.'

Frank let this pass. 'When she first came — you know, when you brought her to the house — I noticed how quiet she was.'

'Certainly she was quiet. One would hardly notice she was in the room.'

'I do notice when she's in the room. But I'd thought that when she'd been with us a little longer, she'd talk more.'

'Of course, as I understood it, she was never expected to stay with you very long.'

'That's my point. I think I ought to know what she intends to do when she leaves here, and whether she has anywhere to go.'

'One could ask her about that, of course. But, Frank, why not leave that task to me? I was responsible, I own, for bringing Lisa to your notice, as I have brought so many unfortunates before her, in the quest for material help. This time, perhaps, you don't feel inclined to thank me.'

'I'm not sure yet whether I do or not,' said Frank. 'I'll tell you later.'

'To return to what you asked me in the first place: do I consider you to be unkind, or to have the potentiality for unkindness? That, Frank, must be a question of the imagination, I mean of picturing the sufferings of others. Now, you're not an imaginative man, Frank. If you have a fault, it's that you don't grasp the importance of what is beyond sense or reason. And yet that is a world in itself. "Where is the stream," we cry, with tears. But look up, and lo! there is the blue stream flowing gently over our heads.'

'I'm not sure whether she trusts me,' said Frank. 'On the whole, I hope not.'

# 22

On the eve of Palm Sunday the servants, in preparation
for their Easter confession, went round the house and
to the neighbours' to ask forgiveness for any sins they
had committed, knowingly or unknowingly, against them.
There was no need to specify the sins.

Frank was taken aback when Lisa told him that she
also needed forgiveness from him, for actions, for words,
and for unspoken thoughts.

'What could you possibly have done wrong?' he asked.
'I don't know what your unspoken thoughts are, but
I've got no complaints about what you do.'

'Who is there who can go through a single day without
doing wrong?'

'Well, if it's going to be a competition, my conscience
isn't clear either.' She waited silently. 'I forgive you, Lisa,'
he said.

On Palm Sunday she put on her black shawl and took
the children out to see the crowds. 'I'll join you later,
I'll look out for you,' he told them. Almost as soon as
they were gone, he was wanted on the telephone. It

was the Ministry of Defence, political division, or more precisely, the Security police.

'We are holding Vladimir Semyonich Grigoriev, a student, who has confessed that he broke into your premises on the night of the 16th of March. Can you identify this man?'

'There are six thousand students in the University,' said Frank.

'But only one of them broke into Reid's Press on the night of the 16th of March, with the aim either of printing subversive matter or of stealing type and other materials in order to print it elsewhere.'

'Nothing was stolen.'

'Why did he go there then? He had the whole of Moscow to choose from. In any case, we are requesting you to come round to Nikitskaya 210, and fetch him away.'

'Fetch him away! It's Palm Sunday: I don't want him!' Frank said. 'I'm always being asked to fetch something or somebody. I'm a printer, not a common carrier.'

'The streets are crowded. You won't be able to get a taxi today. We'll send one for you in six minutes.'

Frank had never been before to the security headquarters on the Nikitskaya, which had nothing to distinguish it from the other four-storey blocks on either side of it. On the third floor, which had none of the carpet-slippered, tobacco-stinking ease of the district police station, he found three men, of whom one did the talking, one took down shorthand notes, and one remained standing by the door. Volodya, looking pitiable, was sitting the wrong way round on a wooden chair, his chin resting on the back. He was wearing his crumpled dark green student's uniform.

Asked to identify the detainee, Frank said he'd never known his surname or his address.

'Well, we do know it,' said the interrogator. 'Can you confirm that your household at 22 Lipka Street consists of yourself and your three legitimate children, a general manservant in charge of opening the door, a cook, an assistant to the cook, a temporary nursery governess whose native village is Vladimir, a yardman, and a boy who formerly cleaned the lamps but now that electricity has been installed, cleans the shoes and does odd jobs of various kinds?' Frank did confirm it, wanting to protest that in spite of the enormity of the list he didn't live as grandly as all that. But it was the way he was expected to live, otherwise he'd be falling short as an employer, just as he was when he shaved himself, instead of going to the barber on the corner of Lipka Street. The interrogator, who had been reading from a card, turned it over and added: 'Your wife Elena Karlovna, has temporarily left you.'

'I don't contest any of this,' said Frank.

The man made a mark on the card, and went on,

'When Grigoriev intruded on your premises, what was it that he intended to print?'

'I don't think it existed, except possibly in his mind.'

'My mind is my own,' cried Volodya, lifting his head from the chair-back. 'You can't touch it.'

No one paid him the slightest attention, a disappointment to Frank, who'd hoped he might be taken away for good.

'Frank Albertovich Reid, we know that you're trying to dispose of your business with the intention of returning to England. During the past eighteen months you have acquired a declaration, made before a notary, that you have no outstanding debts, a police permit declaring that there is no obstacle to your leaving the empire, and a special permit from the Governor General covering the sale of a printing establishment. These documents have been translated into English and you have paid the specified charges for certifying the correctness of the translation and for attesting that it was made by someone authorized by the law of the land to translate it.'

'I don't contest any of that either,' said Frank. 'I'm not leaving Russia at the moment, but I think it's right to be ready to go. All these documents were legally obtained and paid for.'

'And they can be legally invalidated. It won't be so easy to get them a second time.'

'I trust that won't be necessary,' said Frank.

'We are making you a surety for the good behaviour of Vladimir Semyonich Grigoriev. He will be under our surveillance, naturally, but it will be your responsibility to see that he doesn't become involved in any subversive or politically objectionable activity.'

'You haven't forgotten that he broke into my premises?' asked Frank. 'I hadn't pictured myself providing a reference for him.'

'You told me you wished me well,' said Volodya, in a broken voice.

'We shall notify you if Grigoriev changes his address. To recapitulate, if there is any further scandal we shall have to see about the withdrawal of your exit permits, and in any case while Grigoriev is still at the University you will not be in a position to leave Moscow. If you have no further questions, you're free to go now.'

The third officer, who seemed to be there only to open and shut the door, opened it.

# 23

No one had suggested providing a taxi to take them away again, and they walked together through the streets which, after the morning Mass, were emptying themselves towards Red Square. High up and on the edges of the horizon the mists, born of the last snows, became transparent and vanished. The bells rang the entry of Christ into Jerusalem. Frank looked far and near for a sight of Lisa's black shawl. There were hundreds, perhaps thousands of black shawls, and a great many young women in charge of children. She must be there, but she was lost to him.

'Why I didn't turn you in to the police in the first place, I don't know,' he said. 'You've caused me an amazing amount of inconvenience. By the way, who gave you away in the end?'

'I don't understand you,' said Volodya. 'I went to the police myself, I confessed myself, I made a clean breast of it and told them I had broken into your premises.'

Among the crowds, the pedlars of pussy-willow, up from the country, traversed every street, or stood at every

street-corner. By tradition they said nothing to their customers, and, as they held out the red-stalked willows,
named no price. These were grave confrontations. Frank
thought it unlikely that Volodya had any money, and
bought willows for both of them. There was no question
of their going any farther without them.

'Let us forgive each other!' cried Volodya.

'I assure you I'm doing my best,' said Frank.

'You think I'm cracked, perhaps.'

'No, I don't think you're cracked.' Volodya, however,
seemed unwilling to give up the idea. 'At your age, you
were cracked like me.'

'I didn't have time to be cracked,' Frank said. 'It would
be awkward if I were to start now.'

Along the Kremlin wall there were trestle tables, set
out in rows and covered with white cloths. The stall-
holders offered plenty, but not variety. All of them were
selling the same things, and the crowds pressed on, apparently in amazement at the repetition of barrels and jugs
of kvass, strings of bread rolls, kvass, rolls, rolls, kvass.
Frank bought a string of rolls and, not feeling at all
hungry, gave them to Volodya, who began to eat, dang-
ling them from the forefinger of his left hand. He suggested once again that they ought to forgive each other.

'I only want you to remember that to some extent
I'm dependent on your behaviour,' said Frank. 'Let's leave
it at that. I don't think you're dangerous. I'm sure, for

example, that you didn't mean to kill me the other night at my office.'

'Oh, but there you're quite wrong, Frank Albertovich,' said Volodya eagerly. He was still young enough to speak clearly with his mouth full. 'I did mean to kill you. That's what I hadn't explained. I meant to shoot you, but unfortunately there was something wrong with the automatic.'

'I don't know what you mean by "unfortunately" in this connexion,' said Frank, but Volodya rushed on. 'You took Lisa Ivanovna into your house. That was why I tried to kill you.'

'So you're not connected with any political group?'

'No, no.'

'And you didn't want to print anything?'

'No, nothing.'

'Not even a few pages on universal pity?'

'What is universal pity?' asked Volodya doubtfully.

'But you feel responsible for some reason for Lisa Ivanovna, and you wanted to get rid of me. Why didn't you come round to the house and take a shot at me there?'

'That would have caused scandal. For Lisa to be living in the house of a foreign merchant when he was shot might have made things very difficult for her.'

'Lisa works in my house, just as she did at Muir and Merrilees. You never went round there and fired at the manager. Do you seriously think she'll come to any harm with me?'

'I don't know, perhaps not, it makes no difference, I feel like shouting aloud that it's too much for me to bear. Listen, please, I should prefer you to understand. It isn't bearable that she should be approached, spoken to, breathed upon, quite possibly touched by a man such as yourself, Frank Albertovich.'

Volodya was, in fact, shouting aloud, as though addressing one of the forbidden students' meetings. 'Have you ever spoken to her yourself?' Frank asked. Yes, it appeared that Volodya had spoken to her several times, but always in public. He had met her on three separate occasions in the Prechistenskaya public library. He went there because the University libraries were closed during the periods of student unrest, which had become longer and longer. Lisa, after her day behind the counter, went there to read the magazines and newspapers. Speaking in low tones wasn't forbidden in the library, although presumably, Frank reflected, the rules made breathing upon and touching very difficult.

Volodya's eyes were full of unshed tears, which gathered brightly and increased, as Annushka's sometimes did, without a sound. Without warning, dropping the willows and what was left of the bread, he threw his arms round Frank's neck.

'Did you believe what I said? Did you?'

Frank felt outnumbered.

'I didn't want to kill you. When I said that, I wasn't telling the truth. My intention was only to frighten you.'

'What made you think I'd be frightened?'

'I thought you were a coward,' said Volodya, 'but wrongly, wrongly.'

'Why did you think that?'

'Because you ran away from the English governess.'

Frank unhitched Volodya's long clinging arms. He had seen Lisa, Dolly, Ben and Annushka, walking away from him, with their backs to him, past the Inverskaya chapel. Pigeons were threading their way through the press of bodies and legs to retrieve Volodya's fallen bread. Frank hurried across the square, against the human current, towards Lisa. When he caught up with them, (which was not so difficult, after all, since the pavement outside the Inverskaya was laid out in pink and grey granite setts, and Annushka would walk only on the pink ones) the children, with their arms full of willow branches, besieged him. He must agree to their going to the dacha with Lisa for the school holiday, from Easter Tuesday until the Tsaritsa's name day. Frank pointed out that the snow would still be on the ground in the woods, while in Moscow even the windows hadn't been opened yet, and he himself would be wanted at Reidka's, which would not be on holiday. He asked what he was supposed to do without them. Dolly said that she was sure Mrs

Graham would ask him round pretty frequently to the Chaplaincy.

'Swear by the health of His Imperial Majesty that you'll let us go,' shouted Ben.

'But your mother might come back while you're away.'

'Are you expecting her?' Dolly asked.

'No.'

Annushka said she wanted him to carry her. Lisa said nothing. They would, after all, only be away for a few days. However wet and cold they got, it would be unkind not to let them go.

# 24

The sky was of a blue so pale that it could hardly be distinguished from white. On Good Friday the churches stood dark and silent. On Easter Saturday, cheesecakes were brought out in their tens of thousands in every parish, to be blessed. On Monday the house-cleaning began. Every blanket had to be taken outside and beaten, the rugs must come up, the curtains down, fur-lined coats had to be stowed away, the mattresses had to be ripped open and remade, feather by feather. Frank was consulted by Toma as to whether the windows should not be opened. I leave it to you, he said. And the poultry let out? I leave it to you. No post was delivered on Easter Monday, so he went across to fetch it himself from the General Post Office on the west side of the Miasnitskaya. There was nothing from England except an Easter card from Charlie, with a hand-coloured photograph of chickens, lambs and young children, and a printed quotation:

> 'The world would be a dreary place
> Were there no little people in it.'

There was also a letter from Volodya, correctly stamped, which read:

Honoured Frank Albertovich

In my haste on Palm Sunday I am afraid I may not have made myself clear on one point. I may have suggested to you that there was in fact, as well as in possibility, a sexual relationship existing between you and Lisa Ivanovna. Let me say now that having thought more deeply on the subject, and on your reputation in the foreign business community here in Moscow, and particularly on your age, I realize that my suspicions must be groundless. I wish therefore to withdraw them. On every other point in discussion between us my opinions remain the same. Indeed, they are unalterable.

With sincere respects,

Vladimir Semyonich Grigoriev

Although it was not his habit, Frank read the letter through twice. The handwriting, for a student, was wretched.

At 22 Lipka Street packing had already begun for the few days' visit to the dacha. None of the servants were going, though they would have liked to, and to indicate this they had thrown themselves into unnecessary activities, sewing up the children's clothes in rolls of sacking and loading the china into crates of straw. 'We shan't want all these,' said Dolly. It was quite unlike the long summer holiday, when everyone came, and they stocked up as though for a siege. 'There'll be no one there except Egor and Matryona.' She meant the old couple from the nearest village who were supposed to act as caretakers. Toma agreed that there was no point in taking cups and saucers for those who were not able to appreciate them. Those two were born ignorant, he said, and if you boiled them in a kettle for seven years, you wouldn't boil that out of them. 'That's not what I meant at all, Toma, and you know it,' said Dolly. The china remained in the hall, half unpacked again, when night fell.

Frank asked Lisa not to go to bed. 'There's something I want to ask you, and if you're going away for five days I'd better ask you now.'

She stood by the door, untroubled.

'Lisa, do you know a man, a young man, that is, called Volodya Semyonich Grigoriev?'

'Yes, I do. Is he in trouble?'

'Why do you ask that?'

'He's a student,' she said, shrugging her shoulders a little.

Frank wanted to ask her where she had met Volodya, to see if she would tell the same story, but felt this would be base and undignified.

'Where did you meet him?' Lisa asked.

Taken aback, Frank shifted his ground. 'You're quite

right, he has been in trouble. I should be ready to help him, though, if he's a friend of yours.'

Lisa seemed puzzled.

'Would you, Frank Albertovich?'

'No, to be quite honest, I shouldn't.'

'I can't tell what he's been saying about me. What did he say?'

'He told me that he'd only met you three times.'

'Perhaps you could count it as three times, I'm not sure. He used to come into Muir and Merrilees, to the counter, and hang about the department. The students couldn't afford to buy anything. But it was warm in there, and it was also warm in the Prechistenskaya.'

Volodya had written a note, she went on, and put it in the magazine she was reading, then waited while she turned the pages until she got to it. 'That's not such a strange thing in a public library. But you have to write in pencil. When I opened it, it said: "You're alive. I too am alive."'

'I didn't ask you what it said.'

'What kind of trouble is it? I think he's only twenty.'

'And I'm not. That, too, he's pointed out to me.'

Lisa looked at him with polite concern. She seemed, however, as always, to be listening only enough to grasp what was said and to respond to it correctly and efficiently, while compelled to hear, by some inner secret conspiracy, another voice.

'Listen to me, Lisa,' Frank said, gripping her by the forearms, 'since we're telling each other what was in our private correspondence, let me go a bit farther. This Grigoriev told me it wasn't bearable that you should be breathed on, touched, gone near to, spoken to, no, spoken to, breathed on, gone near to, touched, that's it, by a man like me. What do you say to that, Lisa? You're alive. Is it bearable? Is it?'

For the first time he had all her attention, or, if he was deceiving himself there, and I daresay I am, he thought, at least more than he had ever had before. It was the first time, too, that he'd ever made love to a woman with short hair. What an advantage, none of that endless business with the hairpins. And with all the blood in his body he knew that she was not taken by surprise.

'Don't regret this, Frank. If you're sure, if you know beyond any doubt that what you're doing is helpful, then go on, go on with a stout heart.'

It was Selwyn, who must have made his way through the straw and clutter of the front hall. As Frank turned to confront him, Lisa disengaged herself quietly and was out of the room.

'You're angry with me, Frank. But, my old friend, the fathers of the Russian church saw anger itself as "black grace". It helps to remember that. All strong emotions, Frank, may be worthy of grace.'

'Selwyn.'

'Frank, yes.'

'Selwyn, get out of here, if you don't want your teeth down your throat.'

Presumably Selwyn had had some reason for calling, but he had no chance, at that particular moment, to say what it was, while he retreated rapidly towards the front door, Frank went up the dark stairs in to the back of the house and knocked at the door of Lisa's room. He had not expected it to be locked, and it was not locked, but he waited until he heard her bare feet cross the wooden floor to open it.

In the very early morning, they left for Shirokaya. The children said goodbye to him affectionately, but absent-mindedly, the leavers commiserating with the left behind. They had March fever. They were going out of the still sealed-up, glassed up house into the fresh, watery, early spring.

Toma kept repeating that the two taxis which were to take everyone and everything to the station were outside; the drivers had been waiting in the semi-darkness, arguing, for more than an hour. Lisa Ivanovna and the children, Toma said, must sit down for a minute, in the old way, the Russian way, before starting on their journey, to ensure that they'd return safely home. No-one took any notice of him. Blashl, who was never allowed into the house, had floundered into the hall and in her terror was wailing, rather than barking, and wagging her tail insanely. Told to leave, she lost her way and could be heard upturning heavy objects in the kitchen. Lisa appeared in her waterproof.

'What are you going to say to me?' Frank asked her, at the foot of the stairs.

Lisa appeared to think a little and then said, 'Until next Saturday, Frank Albertovich.'

'For God's sake stay with me, Lisa,' said Frank. There was no way of telling whether she had heard him. The doorman and the cook were in the hall to say their goodbyes and Blashl, unrestrained, had trundled once again out of the kitchen quarters, sweeping her tail in wide arcs. Annushka, as disturbed as Blashl by the scent of departures, howled and clung. Lisa restored tranquillity, and in five minutes they were gone. He was almost sure that she could not have heard what he had said to her.

# 25

The dacha was not convenient, and not in good repair. The passionate affection which Dolly and Ben felt for it suggested that, after all, children and adults were hardly of the same species. It was true, though, that Nellie, too, had been unwilling to part with it. And Selwyn, who had no dacha of his own, had often come down for Saturday and Sunday. Oddly enough, when he was there, he behaved much more like an ordinary management accountant than he did in Moscow.

Although there was a large industrial town three miles away, with workers' suburbs and dormitories, Shirokaya could only be reached by a woodcutters' branch-line along the edge of the forest. The nearest village, Ostanovka, got its name from the railway halt. From there the quickest way was on foot through the woods, while the luggage went round by carrier's horse and cart. The carrier also came round twice a week to fill the water-barrels. The rye-bread, heavy as a tombstone, was bought in the village. The tea they brought with them from Moscow.

Tea was drunk with pickled lemons, which stayed in the dacha from one year's end to another in large barrels in the store-room, along with the salted melons, the pears in vinegar, the soused apples, the pickled cabbage, the pickled onions and plums, the pickled mushrooms. The mushrooms, strung from the ceiling, were sorted into the slimy buttery ones, the fleshy rusty ones, the white ones, which were in fact brown, the huge pine-tree ones, the red-capped Aspen ones, the Birch Tree ones, gathered from the north side of the trees, which never dry out. What would have been thought of in Norbury as ordinary mushrooms were despised. They were Unworthy Ones, only strung up and preserved on Frank's account, as he was supposed to like them. The store-room itself was as damp as if it had been beneath the sea. The barrels were made of oak, but they were covered in grey lichen which had never been seen growing on an oak. In Moscow, it was an insult to say of someone that he looked as if he had been scraped off the bath house wall, but moulds and mildews, thicker than in any bath house, spread and flourished among the dacha's stores. Only the strength of the vinegar and vodka, Russia's potent protectors against universal death from poisoning, safe-guarded the unseen fruit and fungus as it brewed through the winter months.

There was a bath house, however, half of the lavatory shed. It worked very simply. Underneath a lid of perforated zinc there was a layer of stones from the brook, which could be heated by lighting a brushwood fire. When the fire had died down you went in, shut the door and pulled back the grating in the roof until Egor's face squinted down at you, ready to pour down a bucket of cold water that raised a suffocating cloud of steam from the blistering heat of the stones. The bath house, Frank knew, ought to be raised a good two feet above the ground, but then, so should the whole place. The damaged planks would have to be cut back until you got to a sound edge, and replaced with sound wood. The sight of the derelict, unkempt dacha, half gone back to moss and earth and almost fermenting with its load of preserves and alcohol would be enough to bring a keen English Saturday carpenter – Charlie, for instance – to the verge of tears.

In front of the dacha, running across its whole length, was a veranda of shaky wooden planks, with a roof supported by fretwork columns. There the day, in summer, when it was hot, could be drowsed away. Courage, though not strength, was needed to raise the loose boards of the flooring. Underneath there was much animal and vegetable life. You could hear a scuttling and rustling, and if you bent down and looked closer you could catch the glint of metal. Some previous tenant, (the whole estate, the forest, the village and the dacha, was owned by a Prince Demidov who preferred to live in Le Touquet) had left his knives and forks there for safety during the winter, and had forgotten them, or perhaps had never returned. And there was part of a croquet set, although who could ever have tried to play croquet at Shirokaya? But thirty years or so ago a croquet set had been the right thing to take down to the country, and perhaps the dacha then had had its own piece of grass.

The forest — as the Prince's German agent had explained to Frank when he first took the lease — had been cleared occasionally, but never cut. The trees grew so close to the dacha that they threw shadows, with the first light, through every window. Only a few yards away from the veranda the forest began. The fringes were of hazel and aspen, with green grass in the clearings as soon as the snow melted, and a wealth of cloudberries, bilberries and wild raspberries. The birches were the true forest. They had created for themselves a deep ground of fallen leaves and seeds, dropped twigs, and rotting bark, decomposing into one of the earth's richest coverings.

As the young birches grew taller the skin at the base of the trunks fragmented and shivered into dark and light patches. The branches showed white against black, black against white. The young twigs were fine and whip-like, dark brown with a purple gloss. As soon as the shining leaf-buds split open the young leaves breathed out an aromatic scent, not so thick as the poplar but wilder and more memorable, the true scent of wild and lonely places. The male catkins appeared in pairs, the pale female catkins followed. The leaves, turning from bright olive to a darker green were agitated and astir even when the wind dropped. They were never strong enough to block out the light completely. The birch forest, unlike the pine forest, always gives a chance of life to whatever grows beneath it.

The spring rain, however welcome, made a complication. The drops ran down the branches as far as the heaviest twig, then hung there perilously, brilliant silver above, dark below. They were tenacious, apparently intending to stay on at all costs. If small birds landed on the branch at the same time, sometimes with the intention of getting at the drops of water, the whole system seemed in jeopardy. Twigs and boughs bent beneath the invasion, sighing, swaying back and forth with a circular motion, crossing and recrossing to settle back into their myriad delicate patterns. And yet quite large birds, starlings and even jackdaws and wood-pigeons, risked the higher branches in the early morning.

In July the fine seed-bracts, pale as meal, were set free from the twigs. The air was full of floating mealy seed. It was useless to try to keep it out of the dacha, all that could be done was to sweep it into weightless mounds in the corner of every room and on the veranda. By autumn, when their aromatic sharpness seemed to have vanished, or rather to have been assimilated into the burial scents of the decaying earth, the birches were hung with yellow leaves, but now the branches seemed too delicate to bear the twigs, the twigs too fragile for the stalks. The long thin fronds seemed to be stretching towards the ground, threatened with exhaustion. In each tree, even in the middle of the forest, there were five or six different movements, from the airy commotion at the top to the stirring of the older branches, often not much thicker than the younger ones, but secure at the dark base. When the heavy autumn rains began the trees gave out a new juicy scent of stewed tea, like the scent of the bundles of birch twigs in the steam-room of a public bath house which the customer used to beat themselves, leaving stray damp leaves on the tingling skin. By early winter the whole forest seemed worn out with the struggle. The clearings were crossed with fallen trunks, here and there, to be stepped over. By the time spring came again they would have sunk into a sepulchre of earth and moss, and beetles innumerable.

There were other dachas in the forest, but they were to the north-west, nearer to the village. At night there was not a light, not a human sound. Egor and Matryona, under their quilt next to the store-room, slept like the dead. There was only the voice of the birch trees.

Sleep walks along the benches, according to the Russian lullaby, and says 'I am sleepy.' Drowsiness says 'I am drowsy.' On the third night, Dolly woke, and knew she had been woken, by the slight noise of a door opening, the door on to the veranda. The noise did not strike her as frightening, rather as something she had been expecting. At home, Blashl would have barked, here there was only the darkness. She put on her boots and school overcoat and went out on to the veranda. Lisa was standing there, leaning against one of the wooden pillars in her waterproof, with her black shawl over her head.

'Are you going out, Lisa?'

'Did you hear the door?'

'Yes, I heard it.'

'It doesn't matter. Yes, I'm going out.'

'Where to?'

'It might have been better if you hadn't woken up, but you did wake up. Now you'll have to come with me.'

She did not take Dolly's hand, or even wait for her, but walked down the veranda steps into the forest. The little girl followed after her, dragging her feet because she had put on her boots without her stockings. She had never been before among the trees at night.

There were paths through the birch forest, made for the autumn shooting. In fact there was a path, which might have been called a ride, almost opposite the dacha. Lisa walked steadily along it, taking the middle of the track, which was raised above the rain-worn hollows on either side. You couldn't say it was pitch-dark. The moon in the cloudy night sky moved among the moving branches. Dolly could see, at first, if she looked back, the light in the dacha front window which was left burning all night. Then, although the path seemed to run quite straight, the light disappeared. The dacha, where Ben and Annushka lay strewn and sleeping, divided from her by sleep, was left behind.

At the point where another track crossed their own, Lisa stood still and looked round.

'Dolly, you're limping.'

'I'm all right.'

'I can't go back with you now.'

'I'm all right.'

Dolly was no longer thinking either of herself or of anything else, being concerned with struggling painfully alone through the plunging half-darkness. The leaf scent pressed in on her. There was nothing else to breathe. They had turned to the left, and walked perhaps almost as far as they had come along the first path from the dacha. Then Dolly began to see on each side of her, among the thronging stems of the birch trees, what looked like human hands, moving to touch each other across the whiteness and blackness.

'Lisa,' she called out, 'I can see hands.'

Lisa stood still again. They were in a clearing into which the moon shone. Dolly saw that by every birch tree, close against the trunk, stood a man or a woman. They stood separately pressing themselves each to their own tree. Then they turned their faces towards Lisa, patches of white against the whiteish bark. Dolly saw now that there were many more of them, deep into the thickness of the wood.

'I have come, but I can't stay,' said Lisa. 'You came, all of you, as far as this on my account. I know that, but I can't stay. As you see, I've had to bring this child with me. If she speaks about this, she won't be believed. If she remembers it, she'll understand in time what she's seen.'

No-one answered her, no one spoke. No one left the protection of the trees, or moved towards them. Lisa, in her usual serene and collected manner, turned, and began to take the same way as before back to the dacha. Dolly, tired to death, trudged after her. Half-way down the main path she saw the familiar light again in the window of the dacha. When they reached it, Lisa sat Dolly down on one of the old cane chairs on the veranda, took off her boots, and rubbed her wet feet dry with her shawl. Neither of them said anything about what had happened. Dolly went to her room and lay down in the large old bed which she shared with Annushka. She could still smell the potent leaf-sap of the birch trees. It was as strong inside the house as out.

# 26

At Lipka Street the hallway had been cleared of straw and litter, the china and clothes which should never have been packed were now unpacked, and Blashl was confined uneasily to the yard. Frank suggested that the windows might be unsealed for the spring, but was told that the children would be disappointed if the Opening took place without them. He wondered by what guile or what process of persuasion he had been led to allow them to go to the half-savage, mouldering dacha in charge of the girl whom he pressingly and achingly needed here in his own house.

'I'll go down and fetch them on Saturday,' he told Toma, who had been forbidden to make any more direct reference to the children. 'Not for three more days! Even your brother-in-law would have been company for you!' cried Toma.

The post arrived. Nothing from England, an invitation from Mrs Graham — just a small party and she'd be glad if he liked to stay on after the others had left — and an official letter from the Ministry of Defence. This was to say that F. A. Reid, a foreign resident, printer and former importer of printing machinery, was released from his responsibility towards V. S. Grigoriev, student of the University of Moscow, who had been taken once again into preventive detention. There would now be no objection, since he held the necessary permits, to the departure of F. A. Reid and his family from the Russian Empire at his earliest convenience.

First they'd wanted him to stop, now they wanted him to go. In spite of himself Frank felt a deep pang at his first rejection from the magnificent and ramshackle country whose history, since he was born, had been his history, and whose future he could scarcely guess at. The Security, of course, might well change their minds again. In a country where nature represented not freedom, but law, where the harbours freed themselves from ice one after another, in majestic sequence, and the earth's harvest failed unfailingly once in every three years, the human authorities proceeded by fits and starts and inexplicable welcomes and withdrawals. To try and work out why they had one opinion of him last week, and another this, would be a squandering of time. One thing, though; if he was in disfavour, it would make it easier to arrange matters for Tvyordov.

On the eve of Palm Sunday Tvyordov had told Frank that he wished to displace himself. He wanted to go to England.

'It's mostly machine-work there now,' Frank told him.

'But they print by hand in Russian.'

Tvyordov had brought out a copy of Tolstoy's *Resurrection* — the first complete edition in Russian, without the censor's cuts. It had been printed by Headley Brothers at 14 Bishopsgate Without, in the east end of London.

'I don't know Headley's personally,' said Frank, 'but I could write to them, if that's where you want to go. Have you read this book?'

'I've looked at the half-title, title page, and end-matter,' said Tvyordov, 'the rest I haven't read.'

'It's a new explanation of the gospels. The resurrection, for those who understand how to change their lives, takes place on this earth. But this edition isn't in legal circulation. In your place I think I'd get rid of it.'

Tvyordov put the book, without regret, into the satchel which he now carried instead of his familiar bag. Frank guessed that *Resurrection* would go into the river, following Volodya's automatic, the white apron and the tools, and becoming part of the shoals of murky waste which night and day were making their devious way down to the Volga.

'Do you think, Frank Albertovich, that I shall have any difficulty in getting an external passport?'

'They don't want skilled craftsmen to leave,' Frank said. 'But on the other hand they're glad to be rid of trouble-makers and political dissidents.'

'I am not a trouble-maker.'

'But you were a union secretary in 1905, and you're still the branch secretary. I think they'll let you go, but I don't know if you'll be able to come back.'

Tvyordov's face was not designed to show much expression, but a kind of iron or wooden disapproval could be detected now. His object had been to earn substantially in England and then to go back to his native village, Evnyak, the place of willows.

'Are there willows there now?' Frank asked him.

Tvyordov thought not. The stream, he believed, was dried up, the landlord had got permission to deflect the water. There had been a pretty wooden hump-backed bridge, but it had been replaced by concrete for the Imperial Motor-Car Reliability Trials of 1911, when Evnyak had been on the official route, from the Baltic to the Black Sea. Changes, yes, but it was his village still. It was there that he wanted to lay his old compositor's bones.

'Possibly I could go to Bishopsgate Without and leave my wife behind for the time being.'

'I shouldn't do that,' said Frank.

Silently he had stored up the history of the bridge at Evnyak to repeat to Ben, who was fanatically interested in the Reliability Trials. At the end of the day he had often found himself quite well supplied with facts and incidents which might possibly be of interest to the children or, when she had still been there, to Nellie. If no-one wanted to listen to them he put them quietly away.

It occurred to him now, as he read the Security's letter, that he had better sign Tvyordov's application at once, and that Selwyn had better be the second recommendation. He took a taxi to the office and got this done. Selwyn, eagerly writing his signature, glad to be asked for help, suggested that after work they should go to the small hall at the Philharmonia and listen together to a programme of Igor Stravinsky. Frank said that it was kind of him, but he didn't feel much like going out. He found it hard, in point of fact, to concentrate on anything except the first night after Lisa came back to him. Selwyn persisted.

'I thought we could have a serious talk in the interval.'

'Surely it's a mistake to go to the Philharmonia to have a serious talk,' said Frank. 'Why don't you come to the house? You know you're always free to come there, or very nearly always.'

'I'd like the setting to be appropriate for what I have to say.'

'You mean it's something that will only sound right in the refreshment room of a concert-hall?'

'Music always makes its effects, Frank.'

The undefended gaps in Frank's mind allowed for a tormenting image of Lisa and, something he hadn't bargained for, a grotesque Volodya, insisting to the Security, by way of a defence, that he too, was alive. His only resource against these thoughts was the work in hand. 'In any case, I want that *Three Men in a Boat* job finished. None of them will be in tomorrow, it's a compulsory holiday for the Tsaritsa's name day.'

'Ah, Frank, poor woman! Poor woman!'

'I can't worry about the Imperial family now. I'm going down to the paper warehouse.'

He looked doubtfully at Selwyn, who seemed exceptionally pale. 'Come to the house this evening.'

Selwyn said 'Let me start by saying that we've often spoken, you and I, about the two sides of man, the spiritual and the material, as though they were divided. What a mistake that is! The two should be indistinguishable, or rather there should be a gradual transformation, until what seems to be material is seen to be nothing of the kind.'

'Selwyn, what are you talking about?'

'About Nellie.'

'I don't see how you can be. Nellie and I are practical people. I thought when I first met her that I'd never known anyone act more sensibly.'

'But you brought her to Holy Russia, Frank, a land of great contrasts.'

'That's where my work was. She knew that, and she didn't object.'

'Russia hasn't changed you, Frank, because you were

born here. But didn't you find that it changed Nellie? Didn't her whole nature become, as they say here, wider? Didn't she talk less about the household, and go more often to Shirokaya?'

'Perhaps a bit more often, I don't know.'

'Nellie was turning towards the spiritual. Unfortunately she couldn't, as yet, distinguish it from the romantic, which casts a false glow over everything it touches. I tried to explain to you, some time ago now, that I had recently been through a period of sexual temptation and trial. You remember that?'

'I'm afraid I don't,' said Frank.

'Nellie saw me in a false glow, my friend.'

'You're raving, Selwyn. She hardly ever said anything about you.'

'Let me tell you what happened. Before her train drew into Mozhaisk I took a point of vantage where I could see it arrive. You know Mozhaisk, you know the great cathedral there, the Cathedral of St Nicholas. Well, not far from there there's a restaurant on the station, the last opportunity for the passengers to get boiling water for their tea before Borodino. A half-an-hour stop. They all got out. I saw your wife and children get out. They were quite unmistakable. That red tam-o'-shanter! Nellie sent the three children to the refreshment room and began looking up and down the platform. A woman looking for someone who doesn't come is a touching

sight, Frank. The little ones came out and she spoke to
them again — spoke earnestly. The porter took out their
boxes and cases from the guard's van, and a rug, I think
a tartan rug. Then Nellie took one long look round,
again in all directions — there was resignation in that
look! — gave what I suppose was money to the stationmaster, and kissed the children. During all this time I
remained where I was. I didn't go forward. I didn't betray
my presence. She waited on the platform until the very
last moment, the third bell, then she climbed back into
her carriage. Still I didn't reveal myself.'

'God give me patience,' said Frank. 'Do you mean you
were supposed to meet her there?'

'It was not I, Frank, who suggested it.'

'But did you meet her or didn't you?'

'I've told you, what I did. I failed the tryst.'

'What tryst?'

'She wanted to go away with me to some more free
and natural place. Perhaps under the sky in forests of
pine and birch, where a man and a woman can join body
and soul and find out what work they have to do in the
world.'

'Why did she send the children back to Moscow?'

'I supposed that, since I had failed her, she didn't want
to take them on with her to Norbury.'

'My God, they'd have been better off in Norbury than
with you in the middle of a forest of pine and birch. All

right, you arranged to meet Nellie off the Berlin train at Mozhaisk. Why didn't you?'

'For many reasons. I had to consider your feelings, the feelings of a true friend. And then, if I left the Press, I was without any definite means of earnings, and I was doubtful about my capacity to support such a large family.'

'I'm beginning to understand it. You got cold feet and left her stranded. Poor Nellie, poor little Nellie, ditched at a hole of a place like Mozhaisk, walking up and down the platform, and you flaming well never turned up. I've put up with a lot this Easter, but I'm damned if I see why Nellie should have to.'

'Frank,' Selwyn cried, holding up his hands in surrender, 'don't descend to violence! Candidly, that was why I thought it would be better to discuss all this in a public place, where you couldn't act violently, even if you wanted to.'

Frank paused. 'Just tell me one thing. Where is Nellie now?'

'She went to Bright Meadows.'

'Where?'

'A Tolstoyan settlement, of which I'd once given her the address. I call it Tolstoyan, although Lev Nicolaievich, I fear, refused to countenance most of such places. But there are handicrafts, vegetable gardening and, I'm sure, music . . .'

'How do you know she went there? Her own brother didn't know her address. She hasn't written, either to me or to her children.'

'Or to me either, Frank.'

'Well then, who told you?'

'I had news from Muriel Kinsman.'

'Miss Kinsman?'

'She undertook to write to me regularly. I recommended her also, you see, to Bright Meadows, as she seemed at a loss, and had very little money.'

'I don't want to talk about Miss Kinsman. What's the address? Come on, what is it?'

'I can give it to you, but I fear it will be of very little use. I heard from Muriel Kinsman this morning, and she tells me that Nellie found she didn't care for the communal life.'

'So she left.'

'Yes, she had left Bright Meadows.'

'Selwyn,' said Frank, with extreme bitterness. 'You could have told me all this before.'

'I did what I could to help you.'

'Yes, you found Lisa for me.'

'I tried more than once to explain my actions to you in detail. I came to your house only a few evenings ago, not criticizing you in any way, nature and humanity are the only standards I recognize, but it was hardly a moment for discussion, you were with Lisa Ivanovna, with your hands on her breasts. But Frank, perhaps you don't want to discuss this incident.'

'I don't mind talking about Lisa, as long as you don't say she's like a birch tree in the wind. She's solid flesh. She's not an incident.'

Selwyn shook his head.

# 27

On the following morning Frank was called to the telephone. 'It's very early, Toma.' 'Yes, sir, but it's someone speaking from the Alexandervoksal.'

The time was just before seven o'clock. 'Mr Reid, for the second time your children are here all by themselves at this station. Could you make it convenient to fetch them at once?'

'I should like to speak to the elder of my two daughters,' said Frank. 'Please fetch her to your office.'

He stood listening for what seemed a very long time to the distant surge and grind of the station, pierced once by a warning bell.

'This is Darya Frantsovna Reid. Do you hear me?'

She spoke clearly, but not with her old decisiveness.

'Yes, I hear you. Dolly, what have you done with Lisa?'

'She came with us to Ostanovka. Then she put us in a carriage in the train to Moscow. We were quite all right.'

'But what did she do?'

'She just turned away and walked down the platform, so we couldn't wave.'

'But Dolly, where is she?'

'She was going to take another train.'

'Where to?'

'*Papashka*, I'm here with Ben and Annushka. What am I supposed to do?'

When he arrived at the Alexandervoksal he found at first only Dolly. Ben had gone to the engine-cleaning shed, Annushka was counting the money with the attendant in the first class ladies' lavatory. Dolly was standing alone outside the stationmaster's office. She clung to him fiercely, sniffing at his spring overcoat, just out of store, like an animal. The two of them clung together.

She would not be parted from him. The two younger ones wanted to go back to the house where they were received like survivors from an earthquake. Dolly came with him to Reidka's, and sat all morning in the customer's chair in his office.

Agafya came up from the tea-place, carrying sugar with her, prepared, as in former days, to indulge the office's princess. When she saw Dolly she stopped, with the brownish-white sugar sticks still in her hand. Seeing that the comedy was over, she put them back in their paper wrapping, and nodded to the pale and silent Dolly.

'She's helping me a bit with the letters,' said Frank, not very convincingly.

'God will make her of use to you,' said Agafya.

After a time he asked Dolly one or two questions, cautiously, not being sure himself how much he wanted to know. Had they locked the doors of the dacha properly, and given the keys to Egor and Matryona? – Oh, yes, all that! – Had they been into the woods? – Yes, they had. – Were the paths wet? – Yes, rather wet. – When Lisa Ivanovna told them to stay in the train and get out at Moscow, did she say where she was going herself. Yes, Berlin. She had to go to Berlin. – Frank asked nothing more about the visit to the dacha either then or ever.

Volodya, thought to be a conspirator, had turned out to be nothing more than a lover. Lisa, who, Frank could have sworn, was a lover, had turned out to be heaven knows what. It was clear enough now why the Security were in favour of his leaving Russia. He had dangerous employees, or one dangerous employee, at least, a dangerous young woman, pretending to be looking after his children. He had let her escape, more likely arranged it. He must, for example, have given her back her papers, without reporting this to the authorities. But whatever they thought now, they hadn't thought it on Palm Sunday, and Frank couldn't imagine who, in all Moscow, could have suggested it to them since then.

By midday, he saw that he must take Dolly home. He told Selwyn and Bernov to carry on. Selwyn unexpectedly shook his hand.

'Remember that what binds us together is the knowledge of the wrongs we have done to one another.'

Bernov, on the other hand, asked if he could come with them in the taxi, if they were getting one, as far as the Alexander Gardens. It was his lunch hour. On the way he took the opportunity to tell them that he was thinking seriously of going to England. No, not for a visit, to emigrate. He had collected most of the necessary forms.

'Bring them in tomorrow, then,' said Frank, feeling as if he were lifting a heavy weight. 'Have you got an address to go to in England?'

Yes, Charlie had told him that he would always find a hearty welcome in Longfellow Road.

Along the river-banks the grass from last year was showing, indescribably seedy, through the drenched earth, and with it the first patches of new grass. Even in Moscow there was the smell of green grass and leaves, inconceivable for the last five months.

At 22 Lipka Street, Annushka came to the front door with Toma, bellowing 'We're opening the windows!' In the hallway, Ben was energetically turning the handle of the 'Amour' gramophone, which a moment later outroared Annushka with the splendid voice of Fyodor Chaliapin.

'We can't wait any longer, sir,' said Toma. 'The ice has been melted for days, the children are back from the country, the fowls must come out of their shed, or they'll become diseased.'

'I left it entirely to you,' said Frank. 'Go ahead.'

The hens, in fact, were already out, stepping delicately about the backyard, alternately stretching out their long necks with dignity and rummaging, with squalid abandon, in the crevices between the brickwork.

It's not true, Frank thought, that she was pretending to look after the children. She did look after them. It's not true that she pretended to make love to me. She did make love to me.

All morning the yardman had been removing the putty from the inner glass, piece by piece, flake by flake. Blashl, frantic at his long disappearance, howled at intervals, but the yardman worked slowly. When all the putty was off, without a scratch from the chisel, he called, lord of the moment, for the scrapings to be brushed away. The space between the outer and inner windows was black with dead flies. They, too, must be removed, and the sills washed down with soft soap. Then with a shout from the triumphant shoecleaning boy at the top of the house to Ben, still in the hall, the outer windows, some terribly stuck, were shaken and rattled till they opened wide. Throughout the winter the house had been deaf, turned inwards, able to listen only to itself. Now the sounds of Moscow broke in, the bells and voices, the cabs and taxis which had gone by all winter unheard like ghosts of themselves, and with the noise came the spring wind, fresher than it felt in the street, blowing in uninterrupted from the northern regions where the frost still lay.

A horse-and-cab pulled up outside. There were still a good few of them left, for those who had time to spare or didn't want to spend too much. Toma, still dusty and splashed with soap and water, ran out, buttoning up his grey jacket as he went. He opened the door, and Nellie walked into the house.